THE RISING MIST

To Vivienne,
Save Urijah!
M.J. Evans

The Rising Mist

The Final Book of The Mist Trilogy

M. J. Evans

M.J. Evans/ Dancing Horse Press
7013 S. Telluride St.
Foxfield, CO 80016

www.dancinghorsepress.com

Publisher's Note: This is a work of fiction. Names, characters, places, and incidents are a product of the author's imagination. Locales and public names are sometimes used for atmospheric purposes. Any resemblance to actual people, living or dead, or to businesses, companies, events, institutions, or locales is completely coincidental.

Ordering Information: Special discounts are available on quantity purchases by corporations, associations, and others. For details, contact the publisher at the address above.

Second Edition

ISBN 978-0-9766168-9-4

Printed in the United States of America

Thank you to all of the readers of

The Mist Trilogy.

I love hearing from you and am
so happy that you have enjoyed
the story thus far.
I hope you love the conclusion
as much!

Greater love hath no man than this,
that a man lay down his
life for his friends.

John 15:13 (KJV)

Contents

— chapter 1 —

wildfire

Flames shot five stories into the air. Gray, billowing clouds of smoke filled the atmosphere and, as they did so, were photographed by NASA's Terra satellite. The black fingers of charred trees were silhouetted against the red-orange glow created by the searing hot flames. Thick smoke, falling ash, and glowing embers filled the sky. Firefighters fought through the day, through the night, and into the next day to try to stop the rampage called the "Station Fire." Set by an arsonist with the gall to start a fire right by the Angeles National Forest Ranger Station off State Highway 2, this fire, pushed by the Santa Ana winds and fed by the tinder-dry trees in the national forest, burned until it destroyed 140,000 acres, over a hundred homes, and caused the death of two humans and innumerable animals. Directly in the path of the fire sat the beautiful community of La Cañada Flintridge.

La Cañada Flintridge was listed as one of the most expensive cities in the land called the United States. Its population of over twenty thousand could boast of having some of the highest incomes per capita in the country. The Dibbles helped to raise the average. Nestled on ten pristine acres on the north side of the Angeles Crest Highway was the home of Ilene and George Dibble. George had made his fortune in the stock market, investing heavily in tech stocks and selling just before the bust in the nineties.

Ilene was a serious equestrian who managed a show stable that provided the home for twenty valuable show horses, their trainers and riders. Ilene was always at the stable by seven in the morning. Driving to the beautiful green and white barn in a golf cart, it took her only a few minutes to go the short distance that separated the stable from the large family home. The roadway to the stable was lined with trees. In front of the barn was a circular garden featuring a large Charles Russell bronze sculpture of a cowboy riding a bucking bronco. The doors to the barn were framed with pots of colorful flowers. It was truly picturesque.

Ilene spent each morning supervising her head groom, Carlos, and his assistants as they provided the morning feeding, cleaned the stalls, and started the daily rotation of 'turn out.' Aisle ways were always swept, tack rooms were neat and clean, with each piece of tack polished and hanging on its rack or hook, brushes and blankets were placed neatly in their grooming boxes. And, of course, the restroom sparkled. Even Ilene's office was tidy and organized, a reflection of the order in Ilene's life. Both the indoor arena and the outdoor arena were raked with a harrow before the first trainers and riders arrived for the day.

Ilene loved the beauty of her riding facility, especially in the mornings when all seemed fresh and new. She loved walking past the stalls and hearing the horses munching contentedly on their breakfast hay. Any horse that put its head over the door was rewarded with a rub on the forehead and a kind word or two while she reached into her pocket to produce a sugar lump.

However, this hot, late-August day was not an ordinary day. Ilene and George had left their home to visit their newest grandson in another state. They left the care of the horses and stable in the normally capable hands of Carlos. Unfortunately, on this day, Carlos had answered the beck and call of a group of old friends. He decided he was entitled to a night on the town after working so hard. He spent the dark hours of the day bar hopping in the City of Angels with his buddies. Conversation centered around sports with little mention of the wildfires that had started wreaking their damage in the San Gabriel Mountains to the east.

In the wee hours of the morning, a wise and sober friend drove him to his apartment at the front end of the Dibble's stable. He helped Carlos onto his bed, removed his shoes, and left him to sleep it off. As the friend squealed the tires of his car around the bronze sculpture, up the drive, and down the tight curves of Highway 2, he had trouble seeing where he was going. Smoke and ash filled the night air. Had he been a bit wiser, he would have turned on the car radio and heard that the entire area around La Cañada Flintridge had been evacuated.

By five in the morning, the flames had leapt over Highway 2 and were working their way through the landscaped gardens of the Dibble estate. The smoke was so dense it was difficult to tell that the sun was beginning to climb over the San Gabriel Mountains. When the sun did arrive, it appeared as a blood red orb struggling to cast its meager light upon the dreary scene. No sunlight was coming in the window of his apartment to awaken Carlos, though in the condition he was in, it was doubtful he would have awakened anyway.

However, in the stable, all twenty horses were very awake and aware of the impending danger. All horses are intensely fearful of fire, and the heavy smoke coming through the windows in their stalls caused them to start panicking.

Some horses started neighing. Others started kicking. Still others reared and bucked. Their natural instinct to flee was constrained by the stalls that penned them in.

Outside, the flames continued their relentless move toward the stable. The recycled concrete that covered the road in front of the barn slowed down their march for just a moment. But the heat soon took its toll on the bronze sculpture and the tractor parked to the side of the barn. Melted metal dripped onto the shriveled and scorched flower garden and over the gravel road. Flames moved down the side of the barn. The winds sent burning embers through the air and into the large hay shed attached to one side of the stable and open on the side facing the advancing fire. With a whooshing sound made by the fire sucking life-giving oxygen, bales of hay went up in flames and became a burning inferno that warped and melted the barn's metal sides, roof, and beams. Trapped inside, the horses' neighs turned to high-pitched screams.

It wasn't the commotion caused by the banging of steel-clad hooves against stall doors nor the screaming of the mares and geldings that awakened Carlos. It was the sudden splash of ice-cold water covering Carlos's face and shoulders that brought him instantly out of his deep slumber. He jerked up, shaking his head and looking frantically first one direction, then the other. An empty pitcher lay on the floor beside his bed. Nothing else seemed out of place. Simultaneously, he heard and smelled the danger around him. He jumped out of his bed, his heart racing. He ran out of his bedroom and across the small living area to the door that connected his apartment to the stable. The door stood ajar. Smoke was rolling in from the barn.

When he stepped into the stable area, he stopped short and looked around. Even through the ever-increasing smoke, he could see all of the stalls in the brightness created by the glowing ceiling lights. Several of the stall doors were already open; others were opening as he watched, seemingly of their own accord. As he stood there watching, the two front doors to the structure opened widely. The horses galloped toward him, heading for the double main doors. Carlos threw himself out of the way and turned to count the horses as they went through. Eighteen, nineteen, twenty! When the last horse veered past him, he ran for the door himself. He stood for a moment in open-mouthed awe as he watched the horses run toward the angry, hungry flames moving toward them. The lead horses slowed to a calm walk as they moved back and forth in front of the wall of fire. This was something completely out of character for horses. Carlos blinked his eyes in shock as he watched the flames part in front of the first horse. The flames literally moved aside, creating a passageway easily wide enough for the horses to negotiate. The entire herd of beautiful show horses galloped through the wall of fire unscathed. Suddenly, coming to his senses, Carlos ran for the opening himself, not even noticing the sharp gravel as it cut his bare feet.

The horses ran up to the main house, which had fortuitously been bypassed by the fire. They crashed through the lattice fence that bordered the backyard and came to a stop on the patio surrounding the swimming pool. All twenty horses settled down immediately. With their reflections bouncing off the floor-to-ceiling windows of the large home, they lowered their heads and calmly began grazing on the lawn. It was impossible to tell that they had just been through a life-threatening ordeal.

Carlos ran until he found the horses. Panting heavily, he skidded to a stop, knotted his eyebrows, and scratched his head. In all his years of working with horses, he had never seen anything that could compare to this. He had anticipated that the horses would continue running, perhaps into the mountains, perhaps down Highway 2. But he never expected them to be standing in the backyard, calmly eating.

****

When the Dibbles received news of the fire threatening their home, they rushed to the airport and talked their way onto the next flight to Los Angeles. Ilene could not be consoled as she fretted and cried, overcome with fear for the safety of the horses. Calls to the house and Carlos had gone unanswered. The couple had no idea what was happening to their home or stable. Were the horses safe? Had they been evacuated? Ilene had to find out.

Back at Los Angeles International Airport, they ran to their car that had been left in the long-term parking lot. They didn't bother to take the time to pick up their luggage. With George's hands tightly gripping the steering wheel and Ilene beside him wringing hers, the worried couple worked their way through the infamous and infuriating traffic of the city. Finally on Highway 2, they wound their way up the hillside. As they reached the turnoff to their home, George slammed on the brakes of their Lexus. Ilene covered a scream with her hand. The entire landscape was charred and smoldering. Hot spots were still feeding on the last of the available vegetation. Tears flowed freely down both their cheeks, and Ilene began shaking uncontrollably as George drove slowly up the narrow drive.

Just as they spun around the last turn, the smoke miraculously parted. There stood their beautiful family home, untouched by the flames. Standing in the front yard was Carlos, rubbing the necks of two of their horses. Ilene let out a scream and jumped out of the car door. "Carlos!"

Carlos turned and greeted her with a toothy grin. Ilene couldn't decide who to hug first, the groom or her horses.

George stepped up to Carlos and roughly shook the young man's hand. Always the businessman, he got right to the point. "The other horses?"

"They're in the backyard," Carlos struggled to respond while the air was being squeezed out of him by Ilene's tight embrace.

"Any injuries?"

"No, they're all fine," Carlos replied.

"The barn?" asked George.

Carlos frowned. He disentangled himself from Ilene's arms and looked down at the ground. Slowly, he shook his head.

Ilene turned to her husband and buried her face in his shoulder as he wrapped his arms around her. Her shoulders shook as she cried tears of both gratitude and grief.

While she cried, buried deeply in the circle of her husband's arms, George looked over her head toward Carlos. "How were you able to rescue all of the horses? Did you have help?"

"I had help," said Carlos, shaking his head. "But I don't know who it was. I couldn't see them."

"Oh, I understand. It was too smoky," said George, jumping to a reasonable conclusion.

"No, that's not it. I could see all right, but there was nothing to see. Something let the horses out of their stalls, opened the barn doors, parted the flames, and led the horses to the safety of the backyard."

"What do you mean by *something*, Carlos?" asked George.

Carlos opened his mouth and then shut it again while shaking his head slowly back and forth. "I can't explain it, but all that happened before I could do a thing. I just watched and followed."

Ilene, hearing the conversation, turned her head first to look at Carlos then back to look up at her husband. Her brow furrowed and she pressed her lips tightly together as the corners of her mouth curved down. Everything Carlos was saying was confusing and she was having trouble absorbing it all.

George rubbed her back as he spoke. "Carlos, you must be suffering from oxygen deprivation and don't remember clearly what went on," said George soothingly. "Perhaps we should have you checked out at the hospital."

"I don't need a hospital. I know what I saw . . . or I guess I should say, *didn't* see. But believe me, what I am telling you is the truth. I could never have gotten all of these horses out of there by myself."

"Well, if you are sure you're all right . . ." said George, realizing he would never be able to convince Carlos of the irrationality of the things he was saying.

"I'm fine. We just need to get these horses taken care of."

"Oh, Carlos," Ilene gushed as she cried. "I will never be able to thank you enough for saving the horses. But most of all, I am thankful that you are safe."

Carlos nodded and looked down at the ground once more. In his heart, he knew that the same source of help that had saved the horses had saved him as well.

Earlier That Day in a Faraway Place:

Mastis, a beautiful, dapple-gray unicorn, galloped into the clearing in the forest of Celestia, where Nick and his unicorn, Lazari, were casually and comfortably enjoying their breakfast. Right behind Mastis came Bethany astride a palomino unicorn named Shema.

Nick and Lazari looked up and smiled. Their smiles were quickly replaced with looks of concern as they recognized the urgency expressed on the faces of their visitors.

"Nicholas, Lazari, come with us immediately," said Mastis.

Without delay, Nick swung up onto Lazari's dark bay back and followed Mastis and Shema, with Bethany astride, into the forest. They took the path that led to the cave that housed the four corners of the earth. As they galloped along, the trees in the forest of Celestia moved out of their way, making the going much easier. From every direction, other unicorns, all members of the Legion of the Unicorn, joined them. Once they left the forest behind, they crossed a wide meadow covered with lush, green grass and wildflowers of all varieties. The band of unicorns had grown to over a hundred in number. All were galloping as quickly as possible toward the cavern. They covered the ground very quickly and without so much as bending a blade of grass or crushing the petal of a flower.

When they reached the area in front of the large cliff that held the entrance to the cave, Mastis stopped. All of the other unicorns followed his lead and halted behind him, though they jostled around to get a better view of their respected leader. From out of the air, several fairies appeared and hovered around Mastis.

Mastis spoke first, addressing a light green fairy. "Junia sent us, Gidoni. She said there is an emergency on the earth." Junia and Gidoni were leaders of the fairies. They were responsible for organizing all of the fairies as they kept track of the animals on earth. They had the stewardship for reporting to the unicorns in Celestia any assistance needed by the animals.

"Yes, Mastis. Thank you for coming so quickly." The tiny fairy, no more than eight inches in height, turned his handsome face toward the large group of unicorns who had been summoned. His pale green wings whirred as they kept him suspended in the air. "Dear members of the Legion of the Unicorn. Many animals are in immediate need of your assistance at this time. In the land called 'California,' ferocious fires are burning out of control. Countless animals, both wild and domestic, will lose their lives unless we can intervene.

Some have already been lost and will need to be brought through the mist."

Two by two, the unicorns were hastily given their assignments. Some were sent to the homes of the humans, others sent to the forest lands. As they were given their responsibilities, they left the group, hurried to the entrance of the cave, and disappeared into it. Nick on Lazari and Bethany on Shema waited anxiously for their assignments. When everyone else was gone, Gidoni finally turned and addressed them.

With deep concern in his eyes, Gidoni said, "There is a stable that is home to twenty horses. Their human is there but unaware of the danger they are in and has left them trapped in their stalls. The fire will reach them very soon. I fear that all of the horses and their caregiver will perish unless you can find a way to save them. You will need to be both brave and clever. Go! Go quickly. Rescue them if you can." Gidoni waved them off.

Without wasting another minute, Lazari leapt forward, nearly unseating Nick, who grabbed a hunk of mane at the last second to steady himself on the unicorn's broad back. With Shema on his heels, they flew like a breath of wind into the cave and through the many beautiful rooms. They slowed their pace only upon arriving in the square room that held the back side of the waterfall.

"Everyone, eat an invisible clover," said Nick. Each one of them placed an invisible clover in their mouth and felt the tingling sensation on their tongue as the flower dissolved.

Once this was completed, they united their minds on their destination. Gidoni had given them a mental picture of where they were going and they concentrated on this. They stepped side-by-side into the warm, white mist at the bottom of the shimmering blue waterfall. Instantaneously, Nick felt the sensation of floating that he had grown accustomed to on his many trips through the mist and back to earth to help the animals. He loved watching the colors of the rainbow swirl around him as he felt the unicorn beneath him lift off the ground. Once the colors began to dim and eventually disappear, he knew they were close to their destination.

After the mist had nearly dissolved, the little group of rescuers found themselves standing on a circular gravel driveway in front of a large and elegant stable. They stepped out of the faint swirl of remaining mist that they called the "Lochtrill" into the predawn darkness that covered this part of the earth. The Lochtrill was the place to which they needed to return when their mission was complete. They all looked around so as to be able to locate the spot again. Directly behind them was a large bronze statue of a cowboy riding a bucking bronco. Around the statue was a beautiful flower garden. Each of them memorized this location.

It had been a lovely, clear morning in Celestia. On earth, the time was just before sunrise, and far from lovely. The air was filled with thick smoke, making breathing uncomfortable and seeing difficult. When they looked behind them once again, they were shocked to see flames of fire leaping from one tree to the next in its relentless advance directly toward them. Bright orange flames shot up the trees, turning them into pillars of fire. The heat was carried on the wind and seemed to be increasing by the second.

"We don't have much time!" said Bethany, panic evident in her voice.

"Bethany, you find the human and get him out. Shema, Lazari, and I will get the horses out," instructed Nick.

Each of them closed their eyes tightly and drew in their light, immediately becoming invisible. Bethany and Nick slid off the backs of their unicorns. The little group of rescuers ran through the smoke and entered the front of the barn. The inside of the barn was dark. Bethany ran to the wall on their right and flipped on every light switch. Immediately, the stable lights came on. Bethany looked around and found the door labeled "Private Residence." "I'll bet he's in here," she said over her shoulder as she opened the door and went in.

The light switches for the apartment were on the right side of the door, and she reached over to switch them on. She ran through the living area and into the bedroom. There, sprawled out on the bed and snoring loudly, was a man. She ran to the side of his bed and started shaking him. Groaning and flailing his arms wildly, the groom rolled over and buried his head under his pillow.

Bethany's heart started beating faster. The smoke was entering the apartment from the open doorway, and she could hear the crackling of the flames getting louder. She ran back into the living area and headed straight for the kitchen. She threw open the cupboards until she found a plastic pitcher. The young unicorn rider whirled around and moved to the refrigerator. Opening the top door, she yanked out a tray of ice and emptied its contents into the pitcher. She dashed to the sink and filled the pitcher with water. As the water reached the top, she grabbed it and ran back to the bedroom. The groom had rolled over and was now sleeping on his back, his mouth open, his arms spread straight out from both sides of his still-clothed body. Bethany leaned over, lifted the pitcher, and poured the entire contents of ice-cold water directly on his face. She stepped back and dropped the pitcher.

With sputtering and loud complaints, the human woke up. He quickly sat up in his bed, used his sleeves to wipe his face, and looked around. Bethany stood silently watching, safe in her invisibility. She noticed him look quizzically at the pitcher on the floor. She continued watching as he became aware of the smoke silently billowing into his room. He suddenly leapt out of bed and headed for the door, crying aloud, "Oh no! Oh please, no!" He ran past her and she followed him as he darted swiftly out of his apartment and into the barn.

Bethany stood beside him just long enough to assess what Nick and the unicorns were doing. While she had been trying to awaken the groom, Nick, Lazari, and Shema had been moving through the barn, sending peace and comfort into the hearts and minds of each horse. The shrill screams and the kicking, snorting, and pawing came to a stop. Nick, taking advantage of his opposable thumbs, ran from stall door to stall door, flipping up the latches and flinging open the doors. On the other side of the barn, Lazari and Shema were pointing their horns at the stall doors and commanding them to open. Each method worked quite well.

Bethany stood for a moment beside Carlos. She could just barely make out the voices of her companions as they instructed the horses in the escape route. She ran to the front barn doors and threw them open just as the first horses dashed out of their stalls and galloped toward the front of the barn.

Bethany heard Nick come through the doors, talking to their unicorns. Though he was unable to see her, Nick could sense Bethany's spirit. He was aware of her presence at the entrance to the barn. They both turned and looked out. The heat from the flames was melting the metal on the sculpture and on a tractor parked beside the barn. The hay barn, attached to the side of the stable, was in flames, and the steel supports were beginning to sag and melt. Clearly, the roof would soon collapse.

"Help me part the flames, Bethany. We'll make a pathway for the horses to get through."

The first horses to exit the barn were milling around on the gravel drive, displaying uncharacteristic calmness. Nick and

Bethany ran past them and right up to the wall of fire. Drawing upon the power within them, they commanded the flames to part. Just as Moses parted the Red Sea, the ocean of fire moved aside in recognition of their power to control the elements. Shema and Lazari spoke calmly to the horses and commanded them to go through the opening. The horses nearest the fire saw the opening in the wall of flames even though they could not see the unicorns that were directing them. With complete trust, they headed straight for the aperture in the barrier of fire. Shema and Lazari took the lead and cantered through first. All twenty horses followed behind them.

Bethany turned back in search of the groom. Seeing him running out of the barn behind the last horse, she stepped in behind him. Nick held the flames at bay until all had passed safely through the gap.

Beyond the wall of fire, the ground and plants were charred black. Each tree looked like spiky black fingers rising up from the ground. Small patches of fire still worked on consuming anything combustible that remained. Behind them, the stable crashed loudly to the ground. Its siding, roof, and structural supports, ravaged by the heat and flames, gave way, and the entire building collapsed. Nick's heart raced as he realized how close they had come to failing. Had the horses been trapped for just a few more minutes, the ball of fire that was once the barn would have been their funeral pyre.

The main body of the fire was now moving on in search of fresh fodder. Lazari and Shema led the horses up the roadway. It was with great relief that they found the home to be intact. The flames had miraculously passed it right by. They guided the horses around to the back, forcing their way through the decorative white lattice fencing, in search of fresh air and shelter from the smoke and blowing embers.

Nick realized immediately that it only took a change in the winds to bring the fire back upon them. He stopped in the roadway and focused all his power on the area around the house. He created an invisible firewall through which the flames, smoke, and burning embers could not pass. Behind the wall, the air was still and clean. Here, the horses and their human were safe and surrounded with a feeling of peace, the last gift their rescuers left for them. The two unicorns and their riders returned to the Lochtrill. Their energy was spent, but their hearts were filled with joy in having been successful in their mission.

chapter 2

work continues

The life of a member of the Legion of the Unicorn was a busy one. No sooner did Nick and Lazari return from rescuing the horses in the fire but they were immediately sent to help the ponies of Chincoteague.

Off the coast of the land called Virginia, in what is called the Atlantic Ocean, are two islands. The outer island is named Assateague. Assateague protects the smaller inner island of Chincoteague. For hundreds of human years, Assateague has been the home of wild birds and a band of wild ponies. Legend has it that the ponies were castaways from a Spanish galleon that crashed on a reef. Once a year, the entire herd of ponies is gathered from all over the island and driven down to Tom's Cove. When the tide is at its lowest, the frightened stallions, mares, and foals are herded across the channel to the island of Chincoteague. The foals are sold at auction and, the next day, the mares and stallions are sent back across the channel for another year to run free on Assateague Island.

It was the Legion of the Unicorn's job to make sure that all the young foals made the swim safely. Under the cover of invisibility, they swam beside the herd, staying clear of the oyster boats keeping the ponies going in the right direction. If a colt or filly started struggling, the unicorns were there to lift it up or encourage it to move forward on its own as they made sure the little, drenched, and tired foal arrived safely on the shore.

Nick and Lazari stepped out of the Lochtrill onto the shore of Assateague Island. "So, this is Assateague Island, home to the wild ponies of Chincoteague," said Nick.

"If it is called Assateague Island, why don't they call them the ponies of Assateague?" asked Lazari.

Nick pointed across the channel. "Across the bay is the Island of Chincoteague. That is where the ponies will be herded when the tide is at its lowest. They keep the herd small by auctioning off some of the ponies to good homes. Then the rest of the ponies will be herded back to this island to spend the year foraging on the island grasses."

A flatbed ferryboat carrying several horses and cowboys cruised across the channel and up to the sandy beach that surrounded the island. Nick and Lazari, still invisible, stood on the shore and watched it glide toward them. The ramp at the end of the boat was lowered, and the cowboys clucked and hooted to get their mounts to jump off of the boat and onto the sand. Once all of the horses were on land, one of the cowboys shouted to the others, "Let's go find those ponies, boys."

The cowboys kicked their horses and whooped and hollered as they galloped up the sand dune bordering the water. The ponies must not have been far, as it was only a few minutes before the heads of several little horses appeared over the top of the ridge. They were followed by the entire herd. The cowboys continued with their hollering to keep the ponies of all colors and sizes in a tight group, pushing them toward the water. The lead ponies jumped into the channel and started swimming. A few foals were hesitant and only went into the water once they saw their mothers swimming away from them. The cowboys waited on the shore, watching as what they thought was the last pony entered the water. However, they didn't notice a little foal that had been left behind, running down the sand dune behind them.

At this point, the cowboys loaded their horses on the ferry, and the boaters took over the herding. The one foal still on the shore was too afraid to enter the water and whinnied loudly and longingly to its mother that was already swimming away. The foal ran back and forth along the beach. No one remained on the beach to help the foal.

Let's go help him, Lazari, said Nick in his thoughts.

Lazari shook his head, sending his mane flying from one side of his neck to the other. *We need to let him figure it out on his own.*

How can you be so cruel? Can't you see how scared the little guy is?

Yes, I see that. But a bird will never fly over the rainbow if it doesn't gather the courage to leave its nest, responded Lazari patiently.

Well, I'm going to go help him, said Nick with determination. Nick leapt off Lazari's back and started to run toward the foal. Lazari bounded forward and stopped in front of him, forcing Nick to bump into the unicorn's invisible body.

"Let me go, Lazari! Let me help him," Nick said out loud.

"He must learn on his own. Once he steps into the water, we will swim beside him to encourage him," responded Lazari.

At that moment, the foal reared up on his gangly hind legs and leapt into the water. Lazari scooped Nick up over his head and onto his back and followed the foal. Unicorn and unicorn rider bounded into the water beside the struggling foal.

"Easy, little one. We are here with you," said Nick.

"Just swim by pretending you are running. You can do it," added Lazari.

The foal became calm and started pumping his legs.

"That's it! That's it! You are doing great!" cheered Nick as the foal pumped his long legs, moving through the water.

"Which mare is your mother?" asked Lazari.

"The one on the edge of the herd just ahead of us," said the little foal.

"We will stay beside you until you catch up with her," said Lazari, his voice calm and comforting.

Lazari, with Nick on his back and the foal beside them madly moving his legs, swam until they reached the mare.

"There you go, little colt. Stay by your mother," said Nick as he reached over and rubbed the foal's fluffy forelock.

The mare turned her head from side to side, searching for whoever had brought her baby to her and who it was that had just spoken. Speaking to her baby while still pumping her legs through the water, she said, "Who brought you to me?"

"I don't know; I couldn't see them. But they took care of me."

Lazari turned away and headed back toward the shore. Nick slapped Lazari on the neck. "Okay, so you were right!"

Lazari smiled and tossed his head up and down, clearly pleased with himself.

Suddenly, a shout for help caught their attention.

Paul Smithwaite was one of those quintessential, salty old fishermen who had lived his entire life fishing the Atlantic coast. Each year he volunteered to help with the pony drive. This year he found himself in the middle of the channel in his skiff. Maybe it was old age and his balance was going, but whatever it was, one moment Paul was standing in his little boat watching the ponies swim, the next his boat was tipping and he was falling into the saltwater. His rubber boots filled with seawater, and he was dragged beneath the surface calling for help just before his face went underwater. He frantically reached down and tried desperately to release himself from the boots that were acting like anchors attached to his feet. He quickly realized he was failing. The pressure of the water in his high rubber boots was too much for him. Lower and lower he sank, dropping through the salty death chamber.

Just as he was ready to resign himself to a watery grave, he was surprised to feel himself being lifted, as though gravity had reversed itself. Something was clearly pushing him up. Once his head broke the surface of the water, he looked all around for his savior. He saw only the other fishermen pointing and laughing at him as he struggled back into his skiff. Once back in the boat, he clutched the sides and looked over into the water. *Something lifted me*, he told himself . . . *but what?* Peering into the water, he saw nothing. Beneath the surface of the water, under the spell of the invisible clover, Nick, on Lazari, swam away.

The ponies completed their swim across the channel and walked onto the shore of Chincoteague Island where they were welcomed by the long, sweet blades of grass that lined the water's edge. Crowds of tourists cheered to welcome the wild ponies.

With the ponies safe and sound on the shore and Paul safely in his skiff, Nick and Lazari returned to the Lochtrill. As soon as the unicorn and his rider stepped through the waterfall that covered the four corners of the earth, their trainer, Mastis, was there. "More work to do?" asked Nick excitedly.

Mastis nodded his head even as Nick knew what the answer would be. "Come with me," Mastis said as he stepped into the pale blue mist. The boy and his unicorn followed.

A train carrying circus animals in a land called Poland had gone off its track. The boxcars that carried the animals lay on their sides or were piled upon one another. The terrified and injured animals cried out in pain. In the dark of night, Mastis, Lazari, and Nick used their powers to control the elements to untangle the train wreckage and free the animals. The dapple-gray Percherons used for vaulting by a troop of talented acrobats were in bad shape. One could not be saved, and Lazari took him to the Lochtrill and to the land behind the mist. Nick and Mastis stayed until the rest of the Percherons were healed of their injuries.

Soon Lazari was back, bringing Shema and Bethany with him. They set to work on the other animals. The large cats, being as agile as they were, came through the crash unscathed. The elephants had not fared so well. Injury after injury had to be mended. One by one, each of the circus animals was either healed or escorted through the Lochtrill to their life in the Animal Kingdom behind the mist.

On their next assignment, the council sent Nick and Lazari to the land called Argentina to heal a broken leg on a polo pony. The groom had mistakenly put a bridle on the mare that had a bit with a curb chain that ran under her chin. This was something the horse had never experienced. In the rush to change horses between play periods called "chuckers," the polo player had neglected to check his tack. When the new chucker began, the rider pulled back on the reins, which caused the curb chain to dig into the mare's chin. Shocked and confused, the horse reared up and fell over onto her side, breaking a bone in her leg. Nick and Lazari arrived to find the rider kneeling over his mare, tears streaming down his face. The mare lay on her side, injured hind leg lifted into the air. Under the cover of invisibility, it took the unicorn and his rider only a minute to heal the bone.

"You are healed now. All is well," said Lazari to the chestnut thoroughbred.

The mare's head came up and looked toward them. Though she could see nothing, she sensed their presence. "Thank you," she whispered before scrambling back onto her feet to the cheers of the polo fans.

On another mission, Lazari and his rider were sent back to Nick's hometown of New York City to heal a gunshot wound on a faithful Morgan, a police horse trying to keep the city safe from criminals. The policeman was patrolling Central Park on his trusty horse when the two partners chanced upon a robbery in progress. The criminals turned and fired their guns, hitting the beautiful bay in the chest and neck. The gelding endured the pain long enough to see the robbers brought to justice. Once his job was done, he crumpled to the ground, blood streaming down his front legs and staining the grass. The policeman called for help, and soon, several of his cohorts were struggling to get the poor injured animal into a van.

Nick and Lazari worked over the horse as it was being carried in the animal ambulance. By the time they arrived at the veterinarian's clinic, the horse walked down the trailer ramp without a single sign of injury.

The pair traveled on to Syracuse, New York, where the Legion of the Unicorn members were assigned to heal a Standardbred, a descendent of the great Rosalind. Rosalind, the Standardbred racing legend, was now a member of the Legion of the Unicorn. Her new name was Sophira. The filly they went to heal had stumbled while harness racing. The horse behind her had not been able to avoid a crash and had gone right over her. Rosalind's great-granddaughter became entangled in the other horse's sulky and was dragged down the track. Sophira, Lazari, and Nick all worked together to heal her many internal and external injuries. A cheer from the racing fans erupted when the mare stood back up on her feet, shook her mane, lifted her head high, and trotted toward the finish line all by herself.

Chapter 3

The Blizzard

Larry Crisp had passed away many years before, leaving Carol to manage their trail riding business in Estes Park, Colorado, without him. Carol's blonde hair had gracefully turned gray, and her smooth skin had wrinkled under the intense Colorado sun. But she continued to care for her herd of trail horses and provide summer work for several wranglers. By early fall, the aspen leaves finished their summer quaking, turned gold, and dropped to the ground, covering the trails with a yellow carpet. Carol knew it was time to close up shop for another season so she could beat the first snowfall out of town. Her ranch hands went back to school or other jobs, and Carol loaded up her stock trailer with her tack and horses. She turned off the water to the cabin and stable, secured the doors, and drove out beneath the ranch entrance sign that stood proudly in the Rocky Mountains just outside the national park.

Adept at pulling a big rig full of horses, she followed Highway 36 through Boulder. She maneuvered her way through the mousetrap, where three major highways all converged on the north end of Denver, and drove south on I-25 as it curved through the city. She exited the freeway at Arapahoe Road and drove east to Highway 83.

Turning south, she headed for her favorite stopping place: Parker Feed. This feed store had been built and run by an immigrant family from Germany since 1971. When the store was first built on the west side of the highway, Parker Road was no more than a narrow, two-lane country road. From the front porch of the store, the family patriarch, Herman, had watched Parker Road get widened and then widened again, until now it was a six-lane thoroughfare with cars zooming by his little store at forty-five miles per hour.

Carol always looked forward to catching up on their lives while they filled her pickup truck and the front of her horse trailer with bags of feed, wood shavings for bedding, and blocks of salt. The storeowners, Herman, Wanda, and their adult children Tom and Debby, loved to gather around the front counter to discuss local and national politics. After paying for her supplies and helping herself to a treat from the ever-present candy bowl, Carol bid her friends farewell for the winter.

"You heard that a storm is coming in," warned Herman in his thick German accent.

"Yeah, I better get going. I need to make it to my ranch before it hits. See you in the spring on my way back up to the park."

"The boys have you loaded up," said Debby with her customary friendly smile on her face. "Drive carefully and take another treat for the road."

"Thanks, I think I will," Carol said with a smile. She popped a hard candy into her mouth, buttoned up her heavy coat, and left the store through the side door.

The seasoned horsewoman climbed into the cab of her truck, drove out of the yard, and merged back onto Parker

Road heading south. She glanced to the southwest. Instead of the usual blue sky forming the backdrop for Pike's Peak, she could see a wall of dark gray clouds moving slowly east. Confident that she had time to make it to her ranch before the snow hit, she turned on talk radio and listened to the current topic of discussion: whether McDonald's should be required to put carrot sticks in their Happy Meals.

The wind that always preceded the snow arrived as she crossed the Palmer Divide. Bouncing balls of tumbleweed blew across the road in front of her truck. She glanced with a wary eye to the west. The dark bank of clouds was continuing its march toward her.

Three hours later Carol pulled under the log entrance that marked the road to her ranch east of Peyton, Colorado. The ranch had been in the family for three generations. Since Larry's passing, Carol had spent a lot of time worrying about what would happen to it when it was her turn to move on. Several developers had offered to take it off her hands for a handsome price. One man even petitioned the state to force her to sell it to him so he could build a private tollway across it. The local ranchers dubbed the idea the "super slab." So far, her health had been good and she had managed to keep both this ranch and her business in Estes Park going. *Besides*, she said to herself, thinking of all the people her small business employed, *people depend on me*. She could easily have added: *And so do the horses.*

Carol decided to unload the horses but leave the feed she had picked up in Parker until the morning. The forecast had been for several inches of snow, but it didn't sound like anything more than she had handled in the past. She unloaded the horses and checked each one to make sure they had made the trip without causing themselves any harm. She turned out the horses in the big pasture, filled the water tank, and watched the herd gallop away, heading for their favorite draw on the far side of the ranch. She smiled. *Horses are so predictable.* She knew just what they would do. They would check to make sure the draw was where they had left it, find shelter under the pinyon pines for the night, and then show up bright and early in the morning, demanding their morning grain and hay. She took in a deep breath of cold air, noticing the unique smell the air has when snow is on the way. With one last look at the western sky, she turned on her heels and headed for the ranch house.

The snow started just before midnight. It fell softly and silently at first. But the wind switched and started blowing in from the north. The east side of the Rocky Mountains formed a wall that directed the wind and snow straight toward her. This changed everything. The whistling and howling filled the darkness of the night, awakening Carol from a deep sleep. She climbed out of bed, pulled back the out-of-date floral print curtains that covered her bedroom window, and looked out. The snow was blowing sideways past the window glass.

She returned to her bed and picked up the television remote from her bedside table. Without turning on the lamp, her deft fingers found the power button and she pressed it. Immediately, the glow from the screen filled the room with an eerie, silver light. Flipping through the channels, she found that the local news was forecasting the "Storm of the Century," while the national news anchors made themselves look foolish as they blamed it on global warming. Carol pressed the power button, and the screen clicked off. She slid down into her bed and pulled the quilt over her sixty-five-year-old shoulders. She told herself that all would be well. The horses would be waiting for her by the gate in the morning. But hers was a restless sleep that night. She dreamt of her horses huddled together against the pinyon pine trees, trying to keep warm.

Out in the storm, two fairies battled the wind as they scanned the countryside for animals in need. Fighting the strong gusts of wind was exhausting, and they had taken several respites in the occasional spruce or pine. At times, the snow piled up on their wings, necessitating a stop to help each other clear it off. It was nights like this that made the job of a fairy far less glamorous than one might suppose. Just before dawn, they found Carol's horses, just as their owner had seen them in her dream, huddled together in the draw on the far side of the ranch. The horses' backs were covered with snow, creating a perfect camouflage. The fairies would have missed them altogether had one horse not chosen that very moment to shake and snort, sending a puff of snow into the air.

Horses have three needs: safety, comfort, and food, in that order. Carol's horses were having their need for safety met in the semi-shelter of the draw and the pinyons. They were doing their best to find some comfort nestled against one another's bodies. Food? None of that was in sight. The horses decided they would just wait out the storm, even without the food. Finding their way back to the barn in this blizzard was out of the question. Horses have very poor depth perception under good conditions. Adding this to the fact that the line between ground and sky was erased by the blinding snow meant that struggling across the plains would require more energy than they wanted to expend.

The fairies flew down and landed lightly on the back of one of the horses. The poor animal didn't even notice they were there until they spoke to him. Horses, being prey animals, have eyes on the sides of their head. This enables them to see in a three hundred and sixty degree circle just by moving their head one way or the other a mere ten degrees. The horse turned his head slightly to the right and saw the fairies on his back.

"Are you okay?" asked one fairy in her high, squeaky voice.

"For now we are. Let's hope this doesn't last long," responded the horse. He was so completely covered with snow, the fairies couldn't even tell what color his emerging winter coat was going to be once it grew in completely.

"We will get help for you," said the second fairy. The other horses lifted their heads slightly and nodded in acknowledgement and appreciation. They lowered their heads, closed their eyes, and settled in to wait. Balls of ice had already formed under their hooves, clinging to the metal shoes that had not yet been removed for the winter. This made even doing nothing but standing still difficult as the horses rolled forward onto their toes and from side to side, straining their tendons.

Meanwhile, in the comfort afforded by the heavy quilts, Carol awoke several times during the night. With the first sign of light, she gave up on sleep, threw back her warm blankets, and went to the window. What she saw made her heart skip a beat. Snow covered the ground, the depth of which she could not determine from her window, but judging from the height of the drifts against the side of the barn, it was extremely deep. She looked in the direction of the fence beside the barn—no horses and no fence. Only the tops of a few fence posts were visible. The wind was continuing to howl, and the snow was pouring out of the gray clouds with a vengeance. Still, she was not concerned. She had her snowmobile tucked away in the barn. This was nothing she couldn't deal with. What was it the Norwegians said? "There is no such thing as bad weather, only bad clothes," she said aloud to no one but herself. She had the clothes.

Carol's concern for her horses caused her to forego her own breakfast. She found her long oilskin coat she had picked up at Down Under Saddle Shop in Denver, slipped on her high rubber boots over thick wool socks, tucked her blue jeans into the tops of her boots, and opened the kitchen door. As soon as she did, she was hit with a blast of frigid air. She had not guessed the temperature would have dropped so low this time of year. October blizzards were not uncommon on the plains of Colorado, but one this cold seemed unusual to Carol. *Maybe I'm just getting old*, she thought.

She stepped out onto the covered porch that the wind had buried with snow. It was then that she became concerned. The snow was as deep as her porch was high. The four board steps to the walkway were completely covered, and the snow was level with her front deck. She lowered her boot into the snow where she thought the first step to be and sank. Falling forward, she landed, face-first in the deep powder. "This is not going to be easy or pleasant," she said aloud in anguish as she half-crawled, half-swam across the snow toward the barn.

The wind swirled around the barn, creating a clearing of snow in front of the door. After she scaled the drift that formed a wall separating her from the old structure, she was able to push aside the barn door and walk in. She reached over to the side wall and flipped the switch. Immediately the overhead lights came on. Carol felt a sense of relief flood her body. *Thank goodness the wind hasn't taken down the power lines*, she thought.

Beams of soft light from the bulbs reflected off the dust that floated in the air. The smell of hay and leather greeted her nostrils. Carol looked around at the empty stalls and nearly wept. *Why didn't I put the horses in the barn last night? It would have made things so much easier*, she scolded herself harshly.

Carol grabbed a shovel and went back out into the blowing snow. With determination, she threw herself into her work. With grunts and groans and straining muscles, she dug a ramp for the snowmobile through the high drift in front of the barn. Looking ahead, she noticed that the snow was so deep her fence was now completely covered. That made one thing easier: she wouldn't have to dig out the gate; she could just ride her snowmobile right over it. She went back into the barn and pulled the snowmobile on its trailer out into the blizzard. She struggled as she slid the heavy machine off the trailer. That finally accomplished, she hooked up a flat-bottom sled and placed a bale of hay on top of it.

Once on the snowmobile, Carol started the loud engine and drove up the snow ramp she had made, noticing that it was already being filled in with blowing snow. She headed across the top of the snow in a southeast direction toward the draw where she was sure she would find her horses.

The driving snow made it impossible for Carol to see anything, and she quickly became disoriented. Her familiar ranch seemed strange and uninviting. She couldn't locate any recognizable landmarks. After two hours of driving around in the blizzard, Carol realized she had no idea where she was, where the horses were, or even what direction she should go to get back to the ranch house. Then things became much worse. The snowmobile sputtered and died.

In her rush to take food to her horses, Carol had not prepared. She had not checked the gas tank. She had not brought along her cell phone. She hadn't even eaten breakfast. The only thing she had going for her was her warm clothing. Sitting on her snowmobile with the wind and snow blowing over her, she folded her arms, bowed her head, and prayed.

****

Nick and Lazari completed their last assignment and walked slowly up to the Lochtrill. Before they had a chance to step into it, they noticed the swirl of mist spinning quickly. Lowering slowly to the ground was Mastis. "The horses belonging to your friend, Carol Crisp, are in trouble," said the beautiful, dapple-gray unicorn as soon as he stepped out of the Lochtrill.

Carol! Nick had not thought about his old friend for a long time. She was the person who had brought Lazari, who at that time was the horse named Jazz, into his life. Now she needed help with her horses. Nick and Lazari would do anything to help her.

Mastis relayed to them the information the fairies had given him. Then he stepped aside so Nick and Lazari could enter the Lochtrill.

When the sparkling dark bay unicorn and his rider stepped out of the Lochtrill on the Colorado prairie, they were blasted with the blowing snow. Shielding themselves from the stinging pellet-like flakes, Lazari floated across the top of the snow toward the huddled herd of horses. His hooves did not even break the surface of the snow. His long tail flowed out behind him. His mane whipped his rider's face as they flew along. It was now almost dusk, and the snow had not relented for nearly twenty hours. The draw where the horses had found shelter was filling up with snow, making movement for both man and beast nearly impossible. But it was nothing a unicorn couldn't handle.

They arrived at the draw from the north side. Lazari spoke to the horses as he carried his rider down the steep side of the ravine. "Be still, my friends. We are here to help you." It had been a full day since the horses had eaten, and they felt weak from hunger, thirst, and the biting cold. They acknowledged the presence of the unicorn with but the slightest lift of their heads and swishes of their tails. Nick and Lazari went to work immediately, bringing food and warmth to the horses.

Suddenly, Nick could feel Carol's spirit and hear her thoughts. "Lazari, we need to hurry. Carol is in worse trouble than these horses. She is out in this storm. We need to find her quickly."

Lazari paused for just one moment. Knowing they had helped humans on other assignments, he felt comfortable the council would approve of this alteration in their tasks. "Then let's locate her immediately," responded Lazari.

When all of the horses were rejuvenated, Nick mounted the one that seemed to be in the best condition and turned it toward the ridge of snow along the northwest edge of the draw. Lazari leaped over all of the hanging heads and took the lead. A bright beam of light shot out from his sparkling horn, separated the snowflakes, and burnt a pathway in the blanket of snow on the ground. Step by step, Lazari led the herd up the side of the draw and across the field of white. Hoof step after hoof step was placed on dry ground. All of the horses followed in a single-file line, nose to tail, just as they did on the trail rides in Rocky Mountain National Park. They shuffled down the narrow path that Lazari's light was creating. The walls of snow on either side of the path varied in height from two to five feet.

Nick continued speaking words of comfort to the shivering horses as they trudged along with heads down and eyelids half closed. As they moved along, however, Nick kept his mind open to Carol's thoughts, using them as a beacon in the storm to direct their path. He had found Bethany the same way when she was being held prisoner in the far reaches of Hasbadana's Dark Kingdom. A sense of both urgency and panic filled Nick's heart, and he wished he could get the horses to move faster.

****

Carol had been waiting for a break in the storm all day. It never came. The gray sky began to turn darker. The aging rancher knew that above the clouds the sun was setting, and she didn't want to spend the night out in this weather. She realized, with a heavy heart, that no one would come looking for her. None of her friends or neighbors even knew she was home from Estes Park. With no food or water to sustain her, Carol decided she had better try to make her way back to the house. She left the snowmobile behind and started struggling through the deep snow. Each step took great effort because her feet kept sinking. She found the easiest way to move was by scooting along on her stomach. While this was not very efficient, she was, at least, able to make some progress. She hoped she was traveling in the right direction.

The darkness settled in. Just as had happened in the daylight, Carol quickly became confused. She could not tell which way she should crawl. She had no idea where she was in relation to her home. She collapsed in the snow and started to cry. She was hungry, cold, and lost. She started to pray again. "I have tried to help myself; now I need Your help."

The beseeching prayers did not go unheard; assistance was on the way. Nick could sense Carol's spirit drawing him toward her. He could feel her pleading for help. While her prayers were not directed to him, he could clearly feel that he was being sent to answer them.

Lazari continued in the lead, melting a pathway through the snow. Nick looked ahead, searching the darkness for any sign of Carol. They came across the empty snowmobile first. Nick's heart beat faster in concern for his friend. *How long will it take us to find her*? he wondered.

Be calm, Lazari whispered to him in his mind, *we will find her*.

Like a lighthouse in the storm, Nick and Lazari radiated a bright light from their bodies. Carol caught a glimpse of the sparkling light as it moved over her. She lifted her head and looked toward it. And just as a lighthouse beckons a ship at sea, she started crawling on top of the snow toward the source of the light.

"Lazari, become invisible. I'll handle this," said Nick. Immediately, the strength of the light was cut in half as Lazari disappeared.

Carol watched as the objects behind the light drew closer and began to take shape. Her mouth dropped in wonder as she beheld a young man riding one of her horses, and the rest of the herd following behind. The light was coming from the boy. How this was possible, she did not know, nor did she care. All she cared about, at this point, was that she was being given the help she had prayed for. She struggled up onto her knees and slowly pushed herself into a standing position, her boots sinking into the snow. She forced herself to greet her rescuer in an upright position. Suddenly, all of the snow around her mysteriously or miraculously disappeared and she was standing on firm ground.

When Nick reached her, he dismounted and stepped up to her. He took both of her hands in his and looked into her eyes. "Carol," he said with a loving smile.

She cocked her head and examined his face, closely through squinted eyes. "Do I know you?"

"Yes. But it was a long time ago."

"How did you find me?"

"You have a very strong spirit," he responded without further explanation. "Now, let us get you home quickly. You are very weak." Nick bent down and scooped her up into his arms. He walked over to the second horse in the line and placed her on its back. She settled in and grasped a hunk of mane. Secure on the back of the horse, she observed in silence as this handsome young man that looked so familiar walked up and swung his leg over the lead horse. She rode behind him and watched in disbelief as the snow in front of his strangely glowing body melted away before him.

As they walked along, Carol studied her rescuer carefully. She noticed his odd clothing and, of all things, his bare feet! He was out in this blizzard without a coat, hat, or gloves . . . and barefoot! Clearly, he was not from around here. *Where, oh where have I seen him before*? she asked herself over and over.

The wind suddenly stopped blowing and the snow stopped falling just as they reached her ranch house. The street lamp that hung from the front of her barn welcomed them home as they walked over the buried gate.

Nick led the group of horses straight into the barn where the stall doors were already open and hay and grain were waiting. "That's funny," said Carol, scratching her head. "I don't remember filling those hay bins." Nick just smiled in response.

Carol turned to face this familiar stranger. "I am very sorry that I don't remember your name. But somehow, it doesn't matter, does it? You came as an answer to my prayers, and that is all I need to know. Thank you. Thank you for saving my horses and me."

Chapter 4

The Lipizzans

The Strauss Waltz filled the air of the elegant arena located on Michaelerplatz in Central Vienna, Austria. The ornate, Baroque-style arena, nearly all white with only touches of gray and tan, was designed by the architect Fischer von Erlach in 1729 under the direction of then-emperor of Austria, Maximilian II. It took nearly six years to build, and the result was stunning. More stunning than a ballroom, this was to be the home of the world's most beautiful dancers: the white Lipizzan stallions. For nearly three hundred years, through times of peace and times of war, the stallions had been trained here and performed here. Only for a brief time during the Second World War had the stallions been secreted away from their home for their own protection.

The music played on as the audience, seated in two balconies between graceful white columns and beneath the overly elaborate ceiling, watched with bated breath. The double quadrille of eight short and stocky white stallions moved through their paces in perfect synchronization. Their riders sitting exactly straight, having been taught to ride with rods sewn into their riding coats, directed their mounts through the classical dressage movements with nearly invisible aids. Collected trots became passage, with the horses lifting their knees and hocks high. With a moment of suspension while covering very little ground, the stallions appeared to hop from one hoof to the other. Passage changed to an extended trot, during which the front legs move way out in front of the horse's shoulders. Two lines of riders crossed the diagonal lines of the arena, taking turns crossing the center of the arena. In the canter the horses easily performed half-passes—moving diagonally across the arena; pirouettes—turning around their haunches while maintaining a canter; and the changes of canter lead at every stride called "tempi" changes. The horses looked like they were joyously skipping to the music.

Each horse was tacked up for the presentation. Their gold-plated double bridles matched their breast collars and cruppers. Their red saddle pads were trimmed in gold braid, the number of rows indicating the rider's level of training, not the horse's. The riders all wore the traditional double-breasted, brown tailcoat, white breeches, black bicorne style hat—the two-cornered hat made famous by Napoleon—and tall black boots that extended over the front of the rider's bent knee.

As the music came to an end, all eight horses and riders turned and rode abreast toward the royal box at the far end of the arena. They halted squarely on cue. Slowly, each rider raised his right hand, and, exactly together, they all removed their bicorne hats, lowered them to their sides, and bowed their heads in salute to the enormous portrait of Emperor Charles VI. This was the salute they performed at the beginning and end of each performance.

The audience applauded enthusiastically, but none more than the four fairies that were watching from the safety of the three grandiose crystal chandeliers that hung over the arena.

This was the last performance of the season, and they had the best seats in the house. As they clapped, their wings fluttered, shaking the crystals and causing them to send out a musical finale.

Each July, after the last performance of the summer, all of the stallions are moved to their country home for a seven-week vacation. No training, no work, just rolling in the fields and going for a hack in the woods. Since a severe thunderstorm was predicted, all the other stallions at the winter stables had already been moved by horse van the short distance to Heldenberg, a one hour and eighteen minute drive to the northwest of the city.

The enormous horse van had returned and, with its two drivers sitting in the semi truck cab, was sitting behind the stables waiting for the completion of the performance. The two stallions that had flawlessly executed the difficult "airs above the ground" earlier in the performance were already loaded and contentedly munching on hay. The drivers hoped to pick up the last eight stallions and deliver them before the storm hit. They kept looking at the darkening sky then back at the stable doors, hoping to get on the road soon.

Suddenly, both cab doors flew open and strong hands grabbed the two drivers, dragging them out of the truck. A cloth was held over their noses and mouths until they both lost consciousness. Their abductors gagged them, bound their hands and feet, and dragged them to the nearly empty hay storage area. "It will be a long time before anyone finds them in there," said one of the men with a laugh.

The four men, all dressed in black, had their heads and faces wrapped with black felt bandages, similar to polo wraps used on a horse's legs. They spoke with Middle Eastern accents. Two of them were carrying guns. All four climbed into the cab of the van. The two with the guns crawled behind the seats, and the other two took their places in the cab. After unwinding the black bandages from their faces, they put on the caps they had removed from the heads of the drivers. One reached up and, with the heel of his handgun, smashed the dome light. In complete darkness, they waited for the rest of the horses.

They didn't have to wait long. The double stable doors opened and, with a groom at each head, the eight stallions—now cooled and rubbed down, their legs covered with red shipping boots and their bodies covered with red and white stable sheets—were led out of the barn and up the ramp into the large horse van. Each horse was placed in a stall and given a flake of hay to enjoy during the ride. The grooms worked quickly but calmly, and the horses responded by being cooperative.

Once every horse was settled, the grooms walked back down the access ramp and, with grunts and groans, lifted the heavy steel ramp up against the opening. The ramp was secured and all windows and doors were checked. Satisfied that the horses were safely loaded, one of the grooms walked up to the cab and, without looking in, banged on the door. "Okay, Hans, take it away."

The diesel engine that had been noisily idling was shifted into gear, and the truck pulled out onto Michaelerplatz and into the darkened night.

****

No one became concerned until the expected travel time of one hour and eighteen minutes had turned into two hours and thirty minutes. At that point, the phone calls between Vienna and Heldenberg began.

"No, they are not here. We sent them off over two hours ago . . . Yes, perhaps you are right, the weather has turned quite nasty . . . Yes, Hans is at the wheel and he is our best driver. I'm sure he is just taking it easy. If there was a problem, he would have contacted me . . . That's right, no news is good news they always say, whoever 'they' are." Rolf, the director of the Spanish Riding School, hung up the phone, confident that all was well with his stallions.

But an hour later when the phone rang again with the unwelcome news that the horse van had still not arrived, panic set in. The director first made a call to the minister of agriculture, Nikolaus Vanlakovich. The minister of agriculture was the government official responsible for all affairs relating to the government-run Spanish Riding School.

"Minister, this is Rolf," said the director, his heart pounding and perspiration beading up on his forehead. "I am sorry to bother you at such a late hour, and I hope it will all be for nothing, but," he paused, "I don't know how to say this . . ."

"Get on with it," was the curt reply.

"We seem to be missing ten of our stallions."

chapter 5

hostages

The vicious storm descended as though it had a score to settle with mankind just as the horse van turned east, heading toward Budapest. The windshield wipers could not keep up with the torrential rain, and the four occupants of the cab were silent as they peered through the splashing water in an effort to keep the big rig on the road.

In the rear of the van, ten beautiful white stallions settled in for the ride. They had been transported before, many times in fact, and had no reason to be concerned. Contentedly they pulled strands of hay out of their hay bags, chewed slowly, and let the rhythm of the moving floor beneath their feet lull them into a satisfied sleep.

Under desirable driving conditions, the two hundred and fifty kilometers between Vienna and Budapest would take two and a half hours. By the time the van reached the Austrian/Hungarian border, it had been nearly that long. But not long enough for the horses to be missed. The van came to a stop at the border checkpoint. The guard, a Lipizzan fan, left the shelter of his kiosk, ducked his head, and ran to the driver's side of the diesel truck.

"Hey, do you have that van full of the stallions?" he asked, quite cheerfully considering the hour and the storm.

"Sure do," the driver replied in a friendly manner.

"Where're you takin' 'em?"

"All the way to Budapest tonight. They're getting restless in there, so we need to hurry this along."

"Oh sure, sure," responded the border guard. "Go ahead. I've seen this van come through before. Take good care of my favorite horses."

"You can count on that!" said the driver with a wave. Once the window of the truck was closed and the rumbling engine was put in gear, the four hijackers burst out in laughter. Two hours later, an all-points bulletin was sent out for all border crossing guards to be on the lookout for the Spanish Riding School's van and its load of priceless stallions. By that time, the truck and trailer had bypassed Budapest and turned south toward the "White City" of Belgrade, the capitol of Serbia.

Belgrade was an ancient city built on the confluence of the Danube and Sava Rivers. Its history was a violent one. The city's strategic location at the crossroads between the West and the Orient meant it was the target of repeated and often successful conquests. Many times, over thousands of years, it had been destroyed and rebuilt. In the earth year of 2006, Belgrade became the capitol of the newly independent country of Serbia. Four hundred kilometers south of Budapest, Belgrade had been selected by the horsenappers as the perfect hideout for their hostages.

After eight hours of travel, the stallions were restless. They were hungry and thirsty. The four men in the cab had seen to their own needs, but while they had been busy planning lives of crime, they had not studied horse husbandry. The horses' needs had not even crossed their minds. To them, the horses were a commodity to be bargained with, nothing more.

They drove the van across the Danube River and entered a warehouse district. After making some tight right and left turns, the driver stopped in front of an old building covered with broken windows on either side of a tall, wide garage door.

"Let them know we're here," commanded the driver to the man in the front passenger seat. The passenger, a short, dark-skinned man with a full beard, opened the door of the cab and jumped to the ground. He disappeared through a broken-down entry door. In a few minutes, the garage door rumbled open on rusted tracks. The driver deftly steered the huge vehicle into the building. With a creak and a crash the garage door came down, concealing the horse van, with its distinctive coat-of-arms painted on the sides, from sight.

Unseen by the men in the cab or the men who had been awaiting their arrival, four tiny fairies darted through one of the broken windows. After watching the splendid final performance, these four fairies had left their viewing stations on the crystal chandeliers high above the arena. They followed the stallions into the stable area and observed with excitement as the grooms rubbed down the eight sweating, white Lipizzans. Carrots and sugar lumps were passed out to each horse in abundance, and each horse was covered with a red and white travel sheet bearing the coat of arms of the ancient riding school. The fairies floated in the air behind the horses as they were led out to the waiting horse van but immediately sensed that something was wrong. Dashing about, it didn't take long for one of the fairies to find the bound and gagged driver and his companion crumpled up in the hay shed.

All through the night, the fairies struggled against the wind and the rain to keep up with the speeding van. Now they were exhausted as they flew into the dilapidated warehouse.

All four of them landed on top of the van and collapsed with fatigue. They heard the four horsenappers leave the cab and walk through a door in the front of the dust-filled cavern that now housed the van and its precious cargo. The men were complaining about how tired they were but congratulating themselves on their successful mission. They were met at the end of the warehouse by four additional men. Together, they walked down a long, narrow hallway. They entered a dusty old office and shut the door behind them. Not one of them thought to check on the horses.

After a few minutes of rest, the fairies worked their way through the open air vents in the roof of the horse van. The odor from the wet shavings and piles of manure was already strong. The horses, though tired, hungry, and thirsty, were, at this point, in surprisingly good shape.

Hours went by and the temperature in the van continued to rise. Though it was out of the hot, summer sun, the limited ventilation and the horses' sweating bodies caused the van to get hotter and hotter. The hay nets were empty, and no additional food or water had been provided to the horses. The poor animals were becoming restless and apprehensive. They tossed their heads and stomped their hooves. They even pinned back their ears and bared their teeth at one another.

Assessing the situation, the fairies decided it was time to take action. Their efforts to keep the stallions calm were becoming less effective, and they knew they needed the help of the unicorns before the situation turned deadly for the horses. Together, the four fairies bid the large horses farewell, assuring them they would return with help. They dashed up through the ceiling vents and out through a broken window in the back of the warehouse. The distance to the Danube River was not far, and it was not difficult to find a swirl of mist, denoting the presence of a Lochtrill through which they could return to

Celestia. They entered the mist, shimmered, and disappeared like a mirage in the hot desert sun.

****

The living room lights in the home of the Austrian Minister of Agriculture, Nikolaus Vanlakovich, were ablaze. Seated on an uncomfortable chair beside the fireplace was Rolf, the director of the Spanish Riding School. All around him were gathered the leaders of the Austrian government, including the head of the government, the federal chancellor. The voices grew in volume as tempers flared, only to stop each time the telephone rang.

A report was received that the van had been seen crossing the border into Hungary. While the guard at the border could not identify the driver, he was sure the picture sent over the Internet of Hans did not match the man he had spoken to. Hans was blond and blue-eyed. The guard was sure that, even through the rain and the darkness, he had seen a dark-haired, dark-skinned man with a middle-eastern accent. The driver had told the border guard that Budapest was their destination.

The next phone call revealed that the search in and around Budapest had turned up nothing.

"How can an entire horse van just disappear into thin air!" yelled Nikolaus Vanlakovich. The minister of agriculture had never been known for his patience nor his winning ways with people.

"I was about to ask you the same thing," responded the federal chancellor in retort. "It seems to me that *you* are the one who lost it!"

"I didn't lose it. It was stolen," the minister replied loudly.

"Who stole it? And just where are our drivers?" asked another parliament member.

As though in a timely response, the phone rang again. Hans and his copilot had been found bound and gagged in the hay shed. Both men were on their way to the hospital and in no condition to be questioned. Nikolaus Vanlakovich was assured that he would be notified as soon as the two men were coherent.

By midmorning, even the breakfast of rolls and cheese had failed to calm the nerves of the people in the living room. No news had been delivered about the whereabouts of the van and the horses. The temperature in Eastern Europe was nearing record levels, matching the tempers of the people pacing around the living room.

"We must keep this out of the news!" yelled the minister of agriculture. "Rolf!"

The director of the Spanish Riding School jumped in his seat. "Y-Yes, Minister?"

"What have you told your people?"

"Only that there has been a delay transporting the horses and that I would get back to them and tell them when to expect the stallions to arrive."

"And they bought that?"

"As far as I know. I've never given them any reason to doubt my word."

The minister looked around the room, carefully examining each occupant. "None of you have leaked a word of this, is that correct?"

All around the room, innocent expressions covered shaking heads.

"All right! Keep it that way! I don't need a bunch of reporters creating a crisis when there is none."

"Not a crisis?" the director of the riding school jumped up from his chair. "Not a crisis? What could possibly be more of a crisis than the disappearance of ten of our most beautiful stallions?" His voice increased in pitch and volume. "Let me remind you that these horses are the national treasure of Austria. They carry the hearts of all Austrians within their chests."

The prime minister stepped over to him. "Yes, yes, Rolf. We understand what you are saying and we are as concerned as you. What the minister is saying is that he does not want to upset our people. Isn't that right, Nikolaus?"

"Of course that is what I meant!" the minister shouted.

Just then, there was a soft knock on the living room door. "Come in!" barked the head of the house.

One of his aides quietly pushed open the door and softly stepped into the room. In his outstretched hand he held a large white envelope.

"What is this?" asked Nickolas.

"A messenger just brought this to the door. He is awaiting your response in the foyer."

Nikolaus Vanlakovich turned the envelope over in his hands. His name was scribbled on the front. Nothing was on the back. All eyes in the room were on him as he placed the finger of his right hand under the flap and ripped open the envelope. Reaching inside, he pulled out a sheet of smooth white paper. In beautiful handwritten script, the minister read the following message:

Dear Minister Vanlakovich,

By this time you have, undoubtedly, learned of the disappearance of your stallions. They are in our care. You have no reason to be concerned for their safety unless you do not meet our demands immediately. To ensure the safe return of the Lippazons, you must pay us $10,000,000 US dollars. You will receive another *letter with instructions in the next forty-eight hours. If you do not follow our demands and instructions, we will dispose of the horses in a less than humane manner.*

Sincerely, TOLOP
The Organization for the Liberation of Oppressed Peoples

For a moment the room was silent. The next moment it erupted in noise as everyone spoke at once. The federal chancellor spoke the loudest. "A ransom? These so-called 'TOLOP' people are demanding a ransom? Don't they know that we don't pay ransoms?"

The director of the Spanish Riding School stepped boldly toward the prime minister, sweat pouring off his forehead. "We don't pay ransoms for people, of course. But these are the Lipizzan Stallions!" he said, grabbing the letter out of the minister's hand. Scanning over it, he added, "These TOLOP people can't even spell 'Lipizzan' correctly. How much are they going to know about taking care of ten stallions?"

"He's right. These horses that they are holding hostage are the symbol of Austria. We can't just let them murder them!" responded a distinguished and unusually sincere member of parliament.

The federal chancellor looked back and forth between the two men. Then he looked around the room at all of the men and women present. They all appeared to be in agreement. Slowly, he nodded his agreement. With a consensus reached, the chancellor turned to the minister. "Nikolaus, let's meet this messenger, shall we?"

The living room door opened silently, and the minister's aide pushed a young boy into the room. "Here is your messenger, Mr. Minister."

The ragged young boy literally shook in his boots as he removed his hat and twisted it in his hands. "Please, sirs. I know not what was in the envelope. The man promised me ten euros if I would deliver it and bring back the response."

"What man was that, my young friend? Can you tell us about him?" asked the director, kindly. He knew how to work with horses and young boys.

"He was dark, that's all I remember. And he spoke with a funny accent."

The rest of the adults in the room knew instinctively to allow Rolf to continue with the questioning and remained silent.

"And where did you meet this man?"

"Why, just around the corner. I was walking to the market and he offered to pay me ten euros if I would deliver that letter," he said, motioning to the envelope on the floor.

"And where were you to meet him with the response?"

"I don't know. He just told me to leave the house and he would find me." He rummaged through his pants pocket and pulled out a few coins. "See?" he said, holding out his hand with the coins in the palm. "He gave me five euros and said he would give me the rest when I delivered your response."

The young boy stood silently quaking in this roomful of intimidating adults. He didn't move from the spot where he stood, his hand still outstretched, revealing the coins.

Rolf's heart melted for the child. He stepped up to him and kneeled down so that he was at eye level with the boy. Reaching into his pocket, Rolf withdrew several of his own euros and placed them gently in the boy's hand. Then he placed both of his hands on either side of the boy's and gently squeezed. "Keep these coins, my boy. And promise me that you will never talk to strangers again."

"I promise, sir. Thank you," said the child, relief written in his eyes and across his brow. The minister called for his aide and instructed him to follow the boy home.

Alone with one another again, the government leaders resumed their discussion.

"We are agreed, then, that we will pay the ransom," stated the federal chancellor.

The entire group mumbled their approval, all but Rolf who nearly shouted it.

That settled, the discussion turned to logistics. They speculated about what the payment requirements might entail and who would be the delivery person. By the end of the day, the government leaders returned to their own homes, emotionally exhausted. Rolf spent a great deal of time on the phone, making excuses to the stable managers in Heldenberg for the stallions' delay. The minister of agriculture spent a great deal of time figuring out which budget item covered ransom payments for horses.

Chapter 6

Ransom

The heat of the day was taking its toll on the ten stallions. Horses have very delicate digestive systems. In the wild, horses eat constantly. The horse's stomach is very small compared to the size of its overall body, so the pattern of constant feeding is just perfect for maintaining health. Horses also require large amounts of water, so they never wander far from a water source, such as a stream or a lake. Domestic horses do best when they are fed two, three, even four times a day, spending a couple of hours peacefully eating hay after each feeding. These horses, too, must have water always available.

The Lipizzan stallions had grown up under the best of circumstances and had never known neglect. Now they found themselves standing in an extremely hot, increasingly soiled metal box with no food or water. Horses, particularly high-strung horses like stallions, can easily become upset when their routine is changed or their basic necessities are not met. This manifests itself in a life-threatening ailment called "colic." Colic is a severe stomachache or abdominal pain and, since horses cannot vomit, it can become fatal. Several of the stallions were already showing early signs of colic. They were restless. They kicked at their stomachs and attempted to turn and bite at their sides. Their short ties kept them from lying down as they wanted to do. As the hours went by, the lack of water and food made the situation grave for all of them, but those who showed signs of colic were in particularly dire circumstances.

The eight members of the group that called themselves The Organization for the Liberation of Oppressed People, who now had the stallions in captivity—the ultimate oppression—were unaware of the danger that the horses were in, either through ignorance or lack of concern. They remained in an old office, seated in front of several electric fans, and continually communicated over cell phones and computers with their counterparts in Vienna and the Middle East. They were out of earshot of the kicking and neighing coming from the horse van in the back of the warehouse.

Cheers went up when the phone call arrived with the news that Nikolaus Vanlakovich had agreed to pay the ransom. Plans were quickly set in place to collect the payment.

****

While the horsenappers celebrated, three unicorns and two riders quietly opened the rickety door to the warehouse. The cavernous room was a virtual oven. Nick and Bethany slid off the backs of their unicorns and ran to the side ramp of the red and white horse van. Latch by latch, they unlocked the steel door and commanded the heavy ramp to silently lower itself to the floor. Humidity and rank odors poured out upon them.

The horse van was designed to carry twelve horses in four rows of three. The ramp opened in the center of the side, and two rows of three horses faced the entrance from both the front and the rear. Behind each front row of three horses was a second row of three. Two of the back stalls were empty at this time.

Mastis, Lazari, and Shema dashed up the ramp and into the trailer. Nick and Bethany followed right behind. What they saw made their hearts ache and their stomachs churn. The stallions all stood with their heads bowed and many with their eyes closed. Some had sweat running off their long, white manes, dripping onto the wood shavings upon which they stood. Others showed the characteristic signs of severe dehydration with a thick lathered sweat, shallow panting, and eyes that were dull and glazed beneath wrinkled eyelids. The most serious were displaying signs of colic, and a few had thumps, where their entire body was racked with mild, rhythmic spasms.

The members of the Legion of the Unicorn knew they needed to act immediately to save the stallions. Just as a hospital will triage the patients to prioritize the seriousness of the illnesses they are facing, the five rescuers did the same. Mastis immediately called forth a gentle breeze to cool the air. Nick and Bethany found buckets in the front of the trailer and called forth water with electrolytes in it and began giving sips of water to each of the horses. Lazari, Salamite, and Mastis moved from one colicky horse to one suffering thumps and then on to the next. The three unicorns began healing the internal illnesses of the stallions by pointing their sparkling horns toward each horse's belly. A ray of light left the tip of their horns and radiated all over each ill stallion's body, bringing both comfort and healing.

When each stallion had sufficiently recovered, Nick and Bethany filled each hay bag with fresh, green alfalfa. With a sparkle and a pop, each pile of steaming manure was eliminated and the odor in the van became sweet and fresh. Each horse was cleaned until he looked as though he was ready for a performance.

As soon as all ten stallions were munching contentedly on their meals, the five members of the Legion of the Unicorn gathered at the bottom of the ramp. Their work had taken a long time and they were exhausted. The legion members had earned a much-deserved rest. The unicorns bent their front legs and lowered themselves to the ground. Nick sat with his back against Lazari's shoulder. Bethany curled up against Shema, her unicorn's neck encircling her.

"So what will the men think when they come to check on the horses?" asked Bethany with a chuckle. Hours later, the sun set with still no sign of a visit from the horsenappers.

****

The doorbell rang at the home of Nikolaus Vanlakovich in Vienna. The sun had just risen in the east and was shining right in his eyes when he opened the door. At first, the minister could not see anything. A tiny voice caused him to look down.

"Please, sir, I have a delivery for you."

Standing on the threshold of his home was a small girl. Her brown hair was in braids, her clothing, while not expensive, was clean. In her hand she held a white envelope, identical in every way to the one he had received two days earlier.

"I assume a dark-skinned, dark-haired man offered you ten euros to deliver this to me?"

"Yes, sir," was the meek reply.

"Thank you, miss. You have done your job." Nikolaus Vanlakovich took the envelope and reentered his house, locking the stately front door behind him. Before he even reached his living room, there was a soft knock on the door. His heart began beating loudly in his chest as he slowly turned around. Guardedly, he stepped forward and peered through the windows that framed the door. Pacing back and forth on the stoop was Rolf. The minister opened the door. "What are you doing here?"

"I have been watching your house, waiting for another delivery." Rolf glanced down at the envelope. "I see it has arrived."

The minister quickly hid the envelope behind his back. "Well, it is of no concern of yours. I must take care of this myself if we are to get the stallions back. Surely you understand."

"The only thing I understand is that my horses have been stolen by evil men who probably have no idea how to care for a mule, let alone ten high-strung stallions!" said Rolf, his voice rising.

"I know how upset you are, Rolf. I am as concerned as you for the welfare of our Lipizzans. However, the thieves have instructed me that I must do this alone," he said as he brought the envelope back to the front and shook it in Rolf's face.

"What does it say? What are you supposed to do?"

"I have not even had a chance to open it yet," said the minister with obvious annoyance.

Rolf stepped back, embarrassed by his display of impatience, and lowered his voice and eyes. "Of course, Minister. I only desire to be of assistance."

Relenting somewhat, Nikolaus Vanlakovich reached out his free hand and patted Rolf on the shoulder. "Of course . . . I understand. But *you* must understand that this is a very delicate situation. In this envelope are my instructions for delivering the ten million U.S. dollars to these monsters. I have been told that when I drop off the instructions for access to the bank account where I have deposited the money, I will be informed as to where the stallions are being held. I have great hopes that the stallions will be unharmed."

"What gives you that hope?"

"Look at it from the thieves' point of view. In normal circumstances when a hostage has been kidnapped, why would the kidnappers harm their hostage?"

Understanding dawned and reflected itself on Rolf's features. "So the hostage won't talk . . . and horses can't talk." For the first time in two days, Rolf felt a sense of hope course through his body.

"Exactly! Not to mention that they are quite large and would be difficult to dispose of," said the minister as he ushered Rolf down the front steps with a pat on the back. "Now let me get about my work, and I promise that I will inform you first when I have the stallions."

Just before noon, a car pulled up to the minister's house. Carrying an attaché case, Nikolaus Vanlakovich, wearing a business suit and sunglasses, stepped out his front door. He turned and carefully inserted the key in both the lock and the deadbolt, tested the door to make sure it was secure, then dashed down the steps and into the waiting car.

Rolf was waiting in a borrowed sedan just half a block away. When the minister's car pulled out into the street, Rolf let two cars go by before he pulled out into the street himself. He followed the large black limousine from a safe distance. The driver turned east and followed the traffic-filled street called Avedikstr to where the avenue ended in front of the Wien Westbahnhof, the Vienna West train station. The minister got out of the car and hurried into the train station. Rolf pulled his car to the side of the busy street, turned it off, and dashed into the station behind Herr Vanlakovich. As he ran, he pulled out his cell phone and called his friend. He told him where he could find his car, promising to pay the parking ticket, and snapped the phone shut.

Rolf entered the crowded train station. People were hustling about trying to catch their trains. He spotted the minister at the ticket booth. Walking quietly past him, he heard Nikolaus Vanlakovich asking for a round-trip ticket to Budapest. Jumping in line behind a crowd of tourists trying to get to Poland, Rolf worked his way up and purchased his own passageway to the Hungarian capital. Staying a safe distance back, Rolf followed the minister of agriculture to the boarding platform. He watched him get onboard the train before jumping on the next car. Trains leaving Westbahnhof for Budapest must back out of the station, and Rolf was disappointed to find himself in front of the minister's car rather than behind it. This made it harder to observe him.

As the train started backing down the track, Rolf heard a female voice call out his name: "Herr Schneider! How wonderful to see you."

Rolf quickly turned around to face the front of the car. Coming up the aisle toward him was Inge Weinholf, one of the few women to ever have been accepted into the Spanish Riding School.

Under normal circumstances, Rolf would have been pleased to see one of his talented and hard-working students. But not today, not under these circumstances.

Rolf stood and stepped out into the aisle to give her the anticipated hug. As he did so, a short man brushed past him, and Rolf fell back into his seat. Inge was right there, beaming down at him.

"What are you doing, Herr Schneider, taking a holiday?"

Rolf stood again. "Uh . . . yes, yes. And you?"

"The same. I just need a few days out of the saddle to see how the rest of the world lives."

"Yes," he chuckled politely. "I feel the same way."

"Are you going to Budapest?"

"Yes, or thereabouts." He could feel the perspiration beading on his forehead.

"Well, perhaps we could get together over lunch. Where are you staying?"

"Oh, uh, I don't know . . . I mean, I didn't check the itinerary . . . I didn't make the arrangements, you see."

"Oh, of course not," the young woman responded as a blush reddened her cheeks. This great riding instructor certainly had more important things to do than to make his own hotel reservations. "Well, let me give you my cell number and you can call me when you arrive at your hotel," she said as she rustled through her handbag and produced a pen and paper.

When Inge finally returned to her seat, Rolf sat back down with a sigh of relief. He could hear Inge and her traveling companions laughing and joking. Their excitement filled the hot train car. He looked around at the other passengers, curious to see if any of them had given any notice to the encounter. All seemed engrossed in their books or iPods. None seemed to be paying any attention to him. Inge and her friends' enthusiasm for the journey was, obviously, not contagious.

When the train pulled into the Wien Meidling Station, Rolf stepped off the train and ran back two cars, ducking below the windows as he dodged the boarding passengers. Once in the new car, he was relieved to find the front seat open. From this position, he was able to see the back of Herr Vanlakovich's well-groomed head. The minister was sitting by himself, appearing to be engrossed in a book. But Rolf noticed that he never turned the page.

Several miles out of the city, the train entered a tunnel. For just a moment, all went black. Rolf heard the rhythmic click of the train wheels become louder as someone opened the train car's door in front of him. When the sun once again illuminated the interior of the car, Nikolaus Vanlakovich stood in front of Rolf, his face red with anger. Shaking his fist, which was holding a cell phone, he spit out, "What do you think you are doing, Rolf? You have ruined everything!"

Confused, Rolf shook his head, "What do you mean, I've ruined everything?"

"Why are you here? I told you to stay home, to stay out of this," the minister hissed through clenched teeth.

"I was just trying to make sure you were safe," responded Rolf, his heart pounding in his chest.

"They know you are here," the minister whispered harshly while his eyes scanned the faces in the train car.

Shocked, Rolf looked around as well. "How could they know that?" he whispered.

"I don't know, but they do. They just called me and said the deal is off. Now they want twenty million U.S. dollars!"

The train ride to Budapest and back to Vienna was a long one while the minister of agriculture fumed and Rolf fretted. *How did they know I was here?* he kept silently asking himself. The train was hot and stuffy on this summer afternoon. It was full of people. Yet, someone in this train knew where his beloved horses were. Someone had been watching him even as he had watched Nikolaus Vanlakovich. Rolf pretended to be sleeping, but all the while he was stealing glances around the train car, peering through his eyelashes. He felt perspiration from his forehead running down the side of his face. He reached into his pants pocket to retrieve the handkerchief he always kept there. But his fingers felt something else. A piece of paper was crumpled in his pocket. Opening his eyes, he pulled out the paper and smoothed out the wrinkles. It was a note. In neat handwriting, like the original demand letter, it read:

Herr Schneider,

If you ever want to see your horses alive, return to your palace and do not come out until summoned.

TOLOP

Without saying a word, he passed the note over to the minister. Nikolaus Vanlakovich took the note, read it, wadded it up, and tossed it back to Rolf. "I couldn't have said it better myself," he said with a snort. "Where did you get this?"

"I found it in my pocket."

"I won't ask you how it got there because I'm sure you don't have any idea."

Rolf nodded with a puzzled look on his face, his forehead wrinkled and his eyebrows knotted. Suddenly, he remembered the man who had pushed him over as he was standing to talk to Inge. He quickly stood up in front of his seat and looked at each passenger in the car. He stepped into the aisle and headed for the door that separated his car from the next.

"Rolf, where are you going?"

"I am going to look for that man who put the note in my pocket," he said over his shoulder as he passed through the door. The clicking noise from the metal train wheels rolling over the metal tracks filled his ears as he stepped between the rail cars. He pushed open the door to the next car and walked in. He paused briefly before walking down the aisle, looking at each passenger even as he searched his memory for any characteristics that would identify the man who had pushed into him. *He was short and his head was down and his skin was . . . dark!*

His search of the train was futile. He just couldn't be sure what the man looked like. "Short and dark-skinned" was just not enough of a description to go by. He returned to his seat, filled with both discouragement and anger. How could he have been so stupid . . . so blind? When they arrived back at Wien Westbahnhof, a livery driver was waiting for Nikolaus Vanlakovich. Rolf had to find his own way home.

chapter 7

Rolf

Two more days passed and the Legion of the Unicorn members who had been sent to care for the Lipizzan stallions still had not seen a human. Had the unicorns not been there, the horses would surely have died by now. As it was, the ten stallions were in excellent condition. Bethany spent much of her time in the van, caressing the soft white muzzles, brushing the long manes and tails, and talking soothingly to the large horses. She assured each horse that all would be well. Nick made sure the tie stalls were kept clean, and Shema and Lazari kept the horses well fed and hydrated.

At nightfall, the day before, Mastis had left to find the Lochtrill on the shores of the Danube River. He returned to Celestia to consult with the Council of the Twelve Ancients. It was not the custom of the unicorns to interfere with human events. Their job was simply to care for the animals. However, since Hasbadana had started his rampage on earth with his mists of darkness, the unicorns had been forced to meddle in the activities of humans several times. But this had always been done with the permission and guidance of the council. In this case, Mastis found himself standing before the council to ask permission to help return the great Lipizzans to their rightful owners.

"You are certain the stallions have been stolen from their rightful owners?" asked Helam.

"That is the report we received from the fairies who watched the horsenapping take place," responded Mastis.

"And you believe the horses' lives are in danger if left with the humans who have taken them?" asked another council member.

"I am certain of it. Had we not arrived when we did, the horses may have already passed behind the mist."

Helam cocked his head to one side. "Are you here making this request because we allowed Nicholas and Lazari to help that woman in the blizzard?"

"Well, that did play a part in my decision. After all, the legion is in a unique situation now that we have allowed two unicorn riders to join its ranks. It is natural, after all, for them to be concerned with human affairs. In addition to that, we do have responsibility for the welfare of the ten stallions," replied Mastis.

After much deliberation, the wise rulers of Celestia came to a conclusion. "The makeup of our body of illustrious unicorns has changed, and we must change with it. In some ways, Hasbadana's actions have necessitated the change. In other ways, our decision to admit humans to our legion has also changed our mission to a great extent," said Helam. They agreed to let Mastis step in and help the Lipizzans return to their owners. Mastis was sent back with the instructions to find a way to save the Lipizzans from what would otherwise be certain death. The only stipulation was that Nick and Bethany were to be the only ones to make contact with the humans.

Mastis wasted no time galloping across Celestia, through flower-strewn fields and lush forests, to the cave that sheltered the four corners of the earth. He dashed through the large rooms and long tunnels, not taking time to acknowledge his fellow legion members who were, likewise, rushing to fulfill their assignments. He entered the familiar square room, deep inside the cave. Without hesitation, he stepped into the warm white mist at the base of one of the four pale blue waterfalls and focused his concentration on his destination: Belgrade, Serbia.

The large, dapple-gray unicorn stepped out of the Lochtrill on the shore of the famous Danube River and immediately withdrew his light to become invisible. It was early morning, and a ragtag human was sleeping along the shores of the river, rolled up in a tattered blanket. Mastis stopped and looked down at the man. "Forgive me, Council," the unicorn whispered before pointing his horn at the man's aging body. A bright beam of light left the tip of Mastis's horn and surrounded the man. The man squirmed and groaned, but when the light faded, rolled up in the blanket was a renewed body, strong and healthy. The man's hair was clean and neatly trimmed. His face was clean shaven. His teeth were now intact and gleaming white. His clothing was pressed and stylish. "There you go, sir. I have given you a new chance at life," said Mastis as he turned and galloped to the nearby warehouse where his cohorts were eagerly awaiting Mastis's return.

****

While Mastis was gone, Nick decided to explore the building and search for the men responsible for bringing the horses here. The members of the Legion of the Unicorn had no idea of the international intrigue they had become involved in.

The fairies had only told them the horses had been stolen. They knew nothing of the ransom demand nor the failed attempt to deliver the money on the train. Nick walked across the expansive concrete floor of the warehouse that held the horse van until he arrived at a small, windowless door at the far end. He closed his eyes and withdrew his light. Placing his hand on the broken doorknob, he slowly opened the door, pausing each time it creaked. When it was open less than a foot, he slipped his body through the doorframe.

Nick found himself in a dirty, littered, junk-strewn hallway with many doors lining both sides. Several of the doors were ajar, revealing small rooms that Nick assumed were once offices. He stood still for a moment, listening for any sound. His keen ears picked up the scurrying of mice and cockroaches and the buzzing of flies and wasps, but nothing else. The talisman around his neck was cool. He was in no danger. He started walking silently down the hall. In his invisible state and with the talisman telling him he had nothing to fear, Nick felt secure moving about, though he was careful not to disturb anything. This was not an easy task, as he had to nimbly negotiate around tipped-over buckets, abandoned tools, and discarded trash. He went from door to door and looked into the small rooms. Seeing nothing of interest, he moved on. At the end of the hall he stepped into a larger room. Food and beverage containers were strewn over the dusty, dirty tables, indicating that humans had been there recently. Several chairs were lying on their backs or sides, telling Nick that the people had left in a hurry, perhaps in a state of agitation.

"Did you find anyone?" asked Bethany when he returned.

Nick shook his head and, with a puzzled expression, said, "We are alone. At least for now." The moment the words left Nick's mouth, the little door to the outside squeaked on its hinges. Nick, Bethany, Lazari, and Shema immediately withdrew their light and became invisible. The four legionnaires walked silently to the end of the horse van where they could scrutinize the entry. The door stood ajar, but there was no sign of whoever had opened it. They waited in silence until they heard the words: "Do not be concerned. It is I." Immediately, Mastis appeared, standing before them in all his sparkling splendor.

With a sigh of relief, both of the unicorns and their riders released their light as well.

"What did the council decide?" queried Lazari. All ears and eyes were on Mastis, eager for his response.

"We have permission to do whatever is necessary to save the stallions."

Joy filled each of their hearts, for they now knew they could use their powers to ensure that the beautiful horses would live to perform again.

"What do you think we should do, Mastis?" asked Bethany.

"I have concluded that you and Nick need to find the Lipizzans' rightful owners and bring them here. Lazari, Shema, and I will continue to protect and care for the stallions until you return."

"And if the horsenappers return before we get back . . . ?" asked Nick.

"We will do whatever is necessary to protect the stallions until you return with their rightful owners. We will not allow the stallions to be removed from this location."

The plan was immediately accepted by all.

Lazari stepped up to Nick and ran his soft muzzle along his rider's cheek while he released a warm breath of air. "Be safe while we are apart. Hurry back. You will find us here eagerly awaiting your return."

Nick threw both his arms around his unicorn's neck and buried his face in the long black mane. "I wish you were coming with me."

"It will be easier for you to travel in the human world without me."

Bethany stepped back into the van to bid the stallions farewell and tell them of her mission. Each stallion expressed his love and gratitude. The largest and oldest of the stallions said in a quiet voice, "Find Rolf. He will know what to do."

Bethany and Nick dashed out the rickety door and headed to the Lochtrill. "Who is Rolf?" asked Nick as they ran.

"I don't know. That was all the stallion said. This Rolf must be responsible for the stallions in some way."

"Let's start by going to Vienna and locating the Lipizzans' stable. Perhaps that is where we will find this man named Rolf."

Traveling via Lochtrill is a complicated process. Each Lochtrill has one destination and one purpose: to return the legion members to Celestia. Nick and Bethany clasped hands and stepped into the faint cone of mist. "Return us to the land behind the mist," commanded Nick. Instantly the two unicorn riders found themselves lifted into the air and spinning in a clockwise direction. With a flash of light, they left Serbia and the Danube River behind.

The moment the swirling rainbows dissipated, they were lowered back to the ground. Their feet touched the stones in the square room, home of the light blue waterfall that covered the four corners of the earth. The two unicorn riders stepped out of the mist, turned, and, still holding tightly to one another's hand, immediately stepped back in. This time, they focused their concentration on Vienna, Austria.

When their feet touched solid ground, the two riders found themselves standing in the center of a circular street. Directly across the street that carried the name Michaelerplatz stood an enormous Renaissance-period building. The structure was four stories high. The central entrance was an arch that extended three stories. On either side of the arch were enormous marble statues. Sun reflected off the patina on the copper roof of the tall dome that crowned the structure.

The construction of the building, called the Stallburg, was originally started in 1559 and was intended to be the home of Maximilian II. However, since it was not completed on time, the emperor made his home elsewhere, and this magnificent building, truly a palace, became the home of seventy-two Lipizzan stallions.

Nick and Bethany looked around to locate the position of the Lochtrill. Satisfied that they could find it once again, they dashed across the busy Michaelerplatz. Unfortunately, both had forgotten about the dangers associated with crossing a busy street full of speeding cars, and their sudden appearance in the street caused several cars to blast on their horns and swerve to avoid hitting them. By the third lane, Nick held up his hand and commanded the car to stop. The driver sat in his car, gripping the steering wheel and staring out the windshield as he watched two sparkling humans cross the street in front of him. *It must be the sun in my eyes*, he thought, to explain the sudden appearance of two radiant bodies. He looked down and checked his car to try to figure out why it had suddenly stopped.

Panting, their hearts racing, Nick and Bethany leaped up onto the curb in front of the Stallburg. They stopped for a moment to catch their breath and let their hearts return to normal.

Bethany was the first to speak. "Have you ever seen anything so beautiful outside of Celestia?" she said, looking up at the palace.

"No, I don't think I have. Austrians certainly have a flare for the elaborate and the extravagant. Let's go find out if anyone is home." The two unicorn riders dashed up to the entrance. A locked gate was pulled across the arched entry. Peeking through the bars of the gate, the two unicorn riders saw only a quiet courtyard. No one was about. Nothing seemed to be underway on this hot summer day.

Nick grasped the gate with both hands and started shaking it. "Hello, is anyone there?" No response. He tried again. "Hello, hello. We are looking for a man named Rolf. Can anyone hear me?"

Bethany gently pushed him aside and focused her concentration on the lock. With a loud click and a clank, the lock came open. Nick smiled at her as he rolled his eyes. The two dashed into the courtyard and began exploring. All exterior doors that entered the building were securely locked . . . no challenge for Bethany. They went from area to area searching for someone that could help them, specifically someone named Rolf.

They made their way to the performance arena. Both of the young riders stood with their mouths agape as they gazed around the ballroom-like arena. Nick felt a thrill as he looked around this famous facility . . . the Mecca for dressage riders. The light bulbs in the three enormous crystal chandeliers were dark, but the crystals were still sparkling from the sunlight streaming through the many tall windows. The surface of the arena was neatly harrowed with no sign of a hoof print. The smell of fresh paint filled the entire room. But no people were present. Nick and Bethany dashed on, exploring the mini-city, a hodgepodge of buildings that had been added onto one another over the centuries. They ran through the stable area, warm-up and training arenas, and tack rooms. Finally, they came upon a group of offices. There, on one of the doors, written in German, was a sign which, after they commanded the letters to change to English, read: Mr. Rolf Schneider, Director.

"Rolf Schneider!" said Bethany. "That's got to be him. He has to be the one the stallion told me to find." They could hear music playing from inside the office. Bethany knocked loudly on the door. The music continued to play, but no one responded.

Bethany reached out her hand and tried the doorknob. It was locked. "Let me," said Nick with a smile. He focused his powers on the lock, and the door immediately popped open. Nick and Bethany stepped inside. The waltz that welcomed them into the room was probably something the horses danced to when they did their dressage performances. It was coming from a CD player on the bookshelf. Nick stepped up to the shelf and pushed the power button, and the lovely music stopped, leaving them in silence. He felt a little sad at the loss of the music once he had turned it off and wondered why he had done that. Glancing at the books on the shelf, he was able to immediately translate their titles to English. Not surprisingly, he quickly located the book *Classical Horsemanship*. This book was written by Alois Podhajsky, an Olympic medalist and the director of the Spanish Riding School from 1939 to 1964. Surrounding this book were many others outlining proper riding and training and even one called *Horses Not to Ride: Broken Bones Waiting to Happen*. Reluctantly pulling himself away from this wealth of knowledge, Nick turned and examined the room.

All around the office were pictures and posters of the great horses and riders from the Spanish Riding School, spanning many years. Bethany was already studying the photos. "Here he is; here's Rolf," she said with excitement, tapping one of the largest pictures.

Nick came up beside her and looked at the picture that had caught her attention. In the elaborate gold frame was a photograph of a tall, handsome young man standing beside a white Lipizzan. He was dressed in the traditional attire: brown, double-breasted tailcoat, white breeches, and tall, shiny black boots. In the crook of his arm he held a black bicorne hat. His name and the date he became the director of the school were engraved on a plaque on the bottom of the frame. Nick leaned forward and studied the man's face. He was not more than forty, his eyes were blue, and his hair was a light brown. He had a high forehead and a square jaw. Nick studied the face carefully until he was sure he would recognize him if he saw him again.

The young unicorn rider turned and continued his examination of the office. A pillow and blanket lay rumpled on a couch on one side of the room. On the other was a paper-strewn desk. Suddenly, Nick turned back to the photograph of Rolf Schneider. He stepped up to it and stared in the man's eyes.

"He's nearby," he said quietly to Bethany.

"What?" she answered, stepping up beside Nick.

"I can sense his presence and hear his thoughts just like I could feel yours when you were a prisoner in the Dark Kingdom. He is distraught and upset. I think I can find him by following the power of his spirit." Nick turned around and stepped out the door of the office. He stopped in the hallway and listened. With confidence, he turned to the left and walked down the hall. Bethany followed close behind.

Nick led her down a short flight of stairs and out through a door at the landing. They stepped into the bright morning sun. Nick stopped to listen again before walking forward, past several buildings and across a street. Directly in front of them was a quaint café. The sign over the door read: "Café Hofburg." Nick turned to Bethany, "He's in there, I am sure of it."

"Then let's go meet him."

Nick and Bethany opened the door to the café. They were immediately greeted by the scent of warm pastries. Their glowing bodies cast a yellow light around the room that was nearly full of people starting their day at this famous little café. All heads turned to look at them. Quickly, Nick searched the faces, looking for the handsome man with blue eyes and a high forehead below light-brown hair. Bethany tugged on his arm and pointed toward a table on the side of the room. Looking at them with curiosity matching that of the other customers was Rolf Schneider.

Why he agreed to follow the two odd strangers out of the safety of the café moments later, the director of the Spanish Riding School didn't know. The strangers were dressed rather peculiarly, and their bodies had an odd way of glowing, even in the dim light of the Café Hofburg. Yet the moment they stepped through the front door, he knew they were seeking him. Something about their presence when they approached him made him feel at peace. Without saying a word, Rolf stood as they approached his table. The two strangers immediately turned and went back out the door, and now he was following them.

Once outside, Nick spoke softly. "You are Rolf Schneider."

"Yes."

"We have come to help you."

"I know."

chapter 8

rescue

Nick, Bethany, and Rolf returned to the solitude of the Stallburg. They went into the director's office. The director's face blushed with embarrassment at the condition of the room. He grabbed the blanket off the couch and hastily folded it. He motioned to them to be seated. Then he hesitated. "Do you sit?"

Nick and Bethany both smiled. "Yes, sir, we do." Nick said as he took Bethany's elbow and guided her over to the newly cleared couch.

"I apologize for the condition of my office. I have been in a bit of a sticky situation of late." He ran his fingers from his forehead back through his hair. "And I haven't been sleeping much." He stopped and looked intently at the two glowing strangers. Their skin literally sparkled as it filled the room with a warm light. "But you know that, don't you?" he said as he cocked his head to the side.

"Please," said Nick as he motioned toward the chair behind the messy desk. "Please sit, sir. We have much to discuss."

Rolf rushed over to his chair and pulled it around to the front of his desk. He didn't feel the need for the protection of the big wooden barrier between himself and the strangers. He wanted to be near them. He moved his chair in front of the couch and sat so close that his knees nearly touched theirs. "Please tell me that you are here about my stallions," he said, leaning forward with his forearms on his thighs.

Bethany smiled warmly. "Yes, Rolf, we are. They sent us to you."

Rolf nearly crumpled over as he burst into tears. Bethany moved off the couch and kneeled in front of him, putting her arms around his shaking shoulders. "Forgive me," he said between his sobs, "but I have been so worried about them."

"Of course," Bethany said to comfort him. "We understand."

"We are going to help you get them back," added Nick.

Rolf took a deep breath before sitting up. Though he couldn't explain what it was, something about these two messengers made him feel safe in their presence. "Tell me what you know and what I need to do."

"The stallions told us to find you," said Bethany again. "They need your help." Rolf didn't even blink at this. Somehow, learning that his visitors could talk to horses didn't come as a surprise to this lifelong horse lover and famous equestrian.

"Now that we have finally found you, we need to work together to figure out the best course of action to take to rescue the stallions," added Nick.

Rolf sat quietly for a moment. Slowly his expression began to change as his mental state transformed from distraught father figure to determined rescuer, from dressage rider to knight in shining armor. He looked at Nick and Bethany with new eyes. "First, tell me where they are."

"Belgrade," answered Nick.

Rolf took in a quick breath. He had never imagined that the horses had been taken so far. He shook his head, blinked his eyes, and slowly let out his breath. "Belgrade," he whispered, still shaking his head. "Are they all right?"

"We left them in very capable hooves, shall we say," said Nick with a smile.

"And the men who stole them . . . ?"

"We have not seen them."

This shocked the director. "Not seen them? Then who has been caring for them?"

"We have," said Bethany with a big smile, her eyes sparkling.

Rolf looked at her with renewed admiration and appreciation. "How will I ever be able to thank you?"

"Our thanks will be the safe return of the stallions," said Nick. "So we need to develop a plan."

"Is the horse van still there?"

"Oh yes, and the horses are still in it," responded Nick.

"Still in it?" asked Rolf, taken aback once again.

"Yes, with all things considered, that is the safest place for them," said Nick.

Bethany jump in. "But they are clean and well fed."

"And we have the power to keep them feeling calm and at peace," added Nick.

"Yes, I sense that you do, and I am grateful for that," Rolf said softly, dropping his chin to his chest and lowering his eyes. His hands slowly rubbed his thighs.

"Rolf," Nick said, and the director lifted his eyes and looked directly at him. "What would you suggest we do to get the stallions back where they belong?"

"Well, you say that the thieves are not there . . ."

"They were not at the time we left."

"Then let's go there and bring them home," said Rolf with determination. Never one to procrastinate once he had made up his mind, Rolf stood up and walked out the door of his office, down the hall, and out the door.

Nick and Bethany followed as Rolf led the way to the Wien Meidling train station. When he approached the ticket booth, the director turned to his companions. "Something tells me you are not riding with me."

Nick smiled warmly. "You are right. We have our own means of transportation. We will meet you in the warehouse district along the Danube."

Once Nick and Bethany saw Rolf board the train to Budapest with the connection to Belgrade in hand, they headed back to the Lochtrill. *We have found Rolf; we are on our way back*, he said to Lazari in his thoughts. *How are things there?*

The men are back, was the hasty response that came into Nick's mind.

****

While Nick and Bethany were sitting in Rolf's office, Lazari, Shema, and Mastis had their own problems to deal with. It was hot and humid within the walls of the deserted warehouse. The three unicorns filled the van with a feeling of peace, keeping the stallions calm and contented. They made sure that the Lipizzans' physical needs were met as well. Suddenly, the quiet was broken as the enormous garage door screeched on its tracks and rattled open. The unicorns, who happened to be inside the trailer tending to the horses, withdrew their lights and became invisible.

Several men from the group that called itself The Organization for the Liberation of Oppressed People came around from the back of the trailer.

"Hey, who opened up the ramp?" yelled one.

"I don't know. Who cares? Let's just get rid of the horses so we can get out of here."

One man jogged up the ramp carrying a black bag. Just as he stepped into the trailer, he was hit by an unseen force. His body flew back and landed with a *humph* at the bottom of the ramp. He lay on the floor clutching his stomach and groaning loudly.

"What the heck are you doing, Akram?" said one of his cohorts as he leaned over him.

The man named Akram could not speak, but he pointed a shaking finger toward the opening as he grunted.

"Oh, this is ridiculous. Give me those needles, Akram. I'll take care of those horses myself," said another as he picked up a black leather satchel from the floor beside his fallen comrade.

The second man marched up the ramp. He paused for a moment at the top of the ramp and peered inside the trailer. Six white faces were looking toward him, their ears pricked forward in curiosity. Each horse stood securely in his stall.

The dark-haired man attempted to step into the trailer. "Oomph!" He let out a loud noise as the air was knocked out of his lungs and he found himself flying backward out of the doorway. He landed with another loud *oomph* next to Akram.

By this time, the other men in the group, being superstitious, were getting scared. They stepped back several yards from the ramp and huddled together while the two men writhed and groaned on the cement floor.

"I don't like what's going on here," said one.

"I have a really bad feeling about this," said another.

"Let's get out of here," said a third.

Suddenly, a beautiful musical sound filled the cavernous room. The men all looked around, trying to make sense of what they were hearing. Finally the sounds congealed into words that they could understand: "I'm sorry, gentlemen, but we cannot let you go anywhere."

The men looked around in panic, clutching each other and moving into a tighter circle. As they watched, eyes wide and mouths open, three bright circles of light appeared in the doorway of the trailer. The balls of light bounced through the air and hit the floor. As they did so, the balls of light burst apart and spread out into a singular circular sheet of shimmering light that moved under all the men. The two men lying on the floor tried desperately to scoot themselves backward in an attempt to get away. The men who were standing clutched one another, frozen in place with fear gripping their hearts. In terror, all the men watched as the sides of the circle rose up around them and enclosed itself over their heads. The men were lifted off the floor and carried nearly to the ceiling. Screaming like children and shouting for help, the men were suspended in the air, like fish in a net.

****

Nick and Bethany hurried back through the Lochtrill that remained silently swirling in the center of the circular Michaelerplatz. The moment their feet touched the stone floor of the cave they turned around and commanded the falls that cover the four corners of the earth to deliver them back to Belgrade. The two unicorn riders were lifted up in the mist and carried through the prisms of light and swirling rainbows until their feet touched down on the shores of the Danube River. They ran toward the warehouses that lined this section of the famous river as it flowed through the old city. In only a few minutes from the time they left Vienna, they were standing in front of the warehouse that housed the stolen Lipizzans. They stopped and looked at the open garage door. The bright sunlight that reflected off the building made it impossible to see inside the dark cavern.

Bethany turned and looked at Nick. "What is happening in there?"

"Let's find out," replied Nick. His talisman was cool against his skin, indicating that he had nothing to be concerned about. But just to be sure, he sent his thoughts to his unicorn. *Lazari, we have returned. Are you all right? Is it safe to reenter the building?*

Instantly, Lazari came galloping silently out of the open doorway and scooped Nick up onto his back. Nick laughed and slapped the unicorn's neck.

"You had a successful trip, I understand," said Lazari once he stopped prancing around.

"Yes," said Nick, still laughing. "We found Rolf, and he is, as we speak, traveling by train to join us."

"What? You didn't let him travel by Lochtrill?" said Mastis with a wink as he stepped regally out of the darkness of the building, bringing his light with him.

Nick looked over at Mastis with a smile and a wink of his eye. He turned his attention back to Lazari. "Lazari, your last message concerned me. You said the men were back."

"Oh, them," the dark bay unicorn said as he chuckled, tossing his amber-colored horn high into the air. "I'm sure they would love to meet you."

Lazari trotted into the warehouse with Nick on his back. Shema watched them enter the building from her post beside the trailer. "Welcome back, my young friends. Welcome back. We have been busy, yes, quite busy indeed, interfering with the human world," the palomino-colored unicorn said cheerfully. She lifted her head and pointed her horn toward the ceiling.

Nick and Bethany looked up. There, suspended from the ceiling in a net made from beams of light, were half a dozen men, clutching the ropes of light like bars on a jail cell. In their native tongue they started yelling down at Nick and Bethany.

"Hey, you! Get us out of here. These crazy horses have us trapped," said one.

"They aren't horses. They're unicorns," responded another.

"There's no such thing as unicorns, you fool!"

"What are you? Blind? What do you think those things coming out of their heads are?"

"And just how do you think we managed to get up here if not by magic?" added a third as he wiggled around to get more comfortable.

Nick and Bethany rolled their eyes at one another and left the men to argue. Nick slipped off Lazari, and the two unicorn riders walked up the ramp and into the trailer to check on the stallions. Bethany greeted each horse with a pat on the neck or a circular rub on the forehead right between their eyes, a place all horses love to be rubbed. Each horse gently blew warm air onto her cheek.

"We found Rolf," she said quietly as she caressed one stallion's velvet-soft muzzle.

"Is he on his way?" said one of the beautiful horses.

"Yes, he should be here soon," answered Nick.

****

Bethany and Nick found Rolf pacing back and forth along the riverfront. They had been delayed by the authorities they had called to collect the thieves. The unicorn riders had had a lot of fun watching the men trying to explain that they had been captured by big unicorns with long horns and glowing bodies. Mastis, Lazari, and Shema watched from the side of the warehouse in a state of invisibility and smiled to themselves. Nick and Bethany managed to convince the police that they had contacted Rolf Schneider and that he was, at this very moment, waiting for the two of them to lead him to the horses.

When Rolf saw Nick and Bethany with a local police officer walking toward him, he sighed with relief. Out from under the influence of Nick's powers to heal and calm, doubts had started to enter his head. The fears that had crept into his head and heart were immediately released in Nick's presence. "There you are! I was afraid you weren't coming."

"We needed some help from the local authorities," responded Nick, cheerfully.

With this sufficing as an introduction, the officer stepped forward. "Are you the director of the Spanish Riding School in Vienna?" he said in broken German.

"I am," said Rolf, pulling out his identification.

Satisfied, the officer stepped back and let the two odd-looking but beautiful teenagers lead them back to the warehouse that concealed the horse van. Joy and anxiety mixed equally in Rolf's heart when he saw the back of the red and white trailer. He left his escorts behind as he rushed around to the side and up the ramp. Nick and Bethany waited at the bottom of the ramp as Rolf went from horse to horse, carefully checking each one. When he reappeared at the top of the ramp, tears were flowing freely down his face. "They are perfect; each one is simply perfect," he said with love and gratitude.

Rolf spent the next several hours leading horses around the parking lot to let them stretch their legs. As he did so, he used his cell phone to call the minister of agriculture and several of his staff to report where he and the stallions were. He spoke with the excitement of a child. The three unicorns remained invisible as they watched, satisfied they had done the right thing when they chose to interfere in the events of the human world.

Nick and Bethany helped Rolf settle the horses in for the long drive back to Vienna. The authorities brought the director the necessary travel papers to cross the borders. Finally, Rolf climbed into the cab, refreshed his memory about how to drive the truck, then started the loud diesel engine. Nick and Bethany waited silently beside the driver's door.

Satisfied that he was ready to go, Rolf opened the window and reached his hand toward the two strangers. Bethany and Nick each took hold of it. "I don't even know your names," he said, fighting back the tears. "And I don't know where you are from. But I will always be grateful that you came to help my horses." Then, in a moment of sudden inspiration he added, "You are their guardian angels, aren't you?"

chapter 9

captives

With the Lipizzan stallions of the Spanish Riding School safely on their way to their well-earned summer vacation in Heldenberg, the three unicorns and the two riders walked slowly back to the Lochtrill on the shores of the Danube River. The fatigue that filled their bodies was balanced by the joy in their hearts. While it was true they had stepped beyond the traditional bounds of the role of the legion, they took comfort in knowing that justice had been served. Within their hearts, each of the five also knew that the traditional role of the legion had been forever changed.

Nick, riding Lazari, entered the Lochtrill first. Lazari rose up on his hind legs and commanded the swirling mist to return them to Celestia. They were immediately lifted off the ground and rotated three times in a clockwise direction. The city of Belgrade and the shores of the Danube River disappeared.

When the swirling mist and colors faded, Lazari's feet touched down on the dry floor of the cave. They stepped out of the white mist at the base of the pale blue waterfall and waited for their companions. Shema and Bethany arrived next. Mastis came through the mist last.

With heads low and eyes half closed, the little group of legionnaires walked through the tunnels and rooms of the cave. They wove in and out of the stalactites and stalagmites without even acknowledging their beauty. When they finally walked through the mouth of the cave, it was nighttime. The moon was always full in Celestia and was casting a bright white light on the foliage, creating what looked like a winter wonderland. Still, Nick and his companions were too tired to even appreciate the exquisiteness of the scene before them.

It took them quite awhile to slowly weave their way through the trees. As they moved along, the trees bowed in respect and empathy to the tired travelers. At last, they arrived in Nick's clearing. He slid off his exhausted mount to bid Shema and Mastis farewell. He walked up to Shema's side. Bethany leaned down and held out her hand. The unicorn rider took hold of her soft, thin hand and held it as he looked into her beautiful, brown eyes. "You did a great job with those stallions, Bethany. I am proud of you."

"And you as well," she responded while she offered a brief smile of affection.

"Until the morning then," he said as he offered a warm smile in return.

"Yes, until the morning," she answered, her tired eyes still managing to twinkle.

Reluctantly, Nick released her hand and went into his cottage where he heard Lazari already nestling into his straw bed. Nick slipped out of his white tunic and tan pants and stepped into the always-warm pool in the corner of his room. He let the water soak away the ache in his tired muscles as he looked up at the slowly spinning crystal mobile that hung above his head. His eyes watched the tiny rainbows bounce around the room as the crystals sent their internal light all around him. He thought about their latest rescue mission and smiled. He had learned to love serving the animals, and this had been a particularly heartwarming experience. As he thought of the sight of the thieves hanging from the ceiling in the net made from beams of light, he laughed aloud.

You're still awake? he heard Lazari say in his thoughts.

Yes, sorry to disturb you. I was just thinking about how funny those men looked hanging from the ceiling.

Yes. That was Mastis's idea, of course. It was quite clever, wasn't it?

I wonder what tomorrow shall bring, thought Nick, changing the subject. He wondered if they would be on a new adventure on earth or . . .

Tomorrow has a way of taking care of itself, responded Lazari.

****

The morning arrived all too early. Nicholas was awakened by a fairy whom he had not met before.

"Nicholas, oh great unicorn rider. I have been sent by Urijah. He asks that you come to the meadow in front of the council chambers immediately. Apparently there is an emergency," said the little purple fairy.

Nick rubbed his eyes and stretched. It seemed he was always being awakened due to some sort of emergency. However, something in the tone of this fairy's voice told him this was not your usual injured animal that needed help. He dressed quickly, mounted his unicorn, and dashed out of his forest clearing toward the council chambers. Halfway there, they were joined by Bethany on Shema.

Urijah, the Lord of Celestia, their trainer, Mastis, and Helam, a member of the Council of the Twelve Ancients, were waiting for them in front of the golden doors that marked the entrance to the council chambers. Urijah's magnificence filled the entire meadow. The great, sparkling white unicorn radiated the power of love, and every living thing relished being in his presence, drawing strength just by being near him. Every unicorn present in the meadow was now kneeling before this lord of the light to show their respect. Every tree, flower, and blade of grass bowed to him.

Nick and Bethany leapt off their unicorns and bent at the waist to show both their respect and admiration for this great unicorn. But for both Nick and Bethany, it was more than that. They wanted to show their love for him as well. Lazari and Shema greeted Urijah, Mastis, and Helam in the traditional unicorn fashion by touching their muzzles and blowing out a warm breath of air, then lowering their heads and touching their horns to the ground.

Urijah, Mastis, and Helam greeted them warmly, but Nick noticed a look of concern on their beautiful faces. Urijah spoke first. "Nicholas, we have called you here to deliver some disturbing news."

Nick cocked his head to one side. He couldn't presume to even guess what the news could be that would be so terrible that the Lord of Celestia felt moved to deliver it himself.

Urijah stepped up to Nick and rubbed his cheek with his muzzle. Immediately, Nick was infused with a warm sense of well-being. Urijah stepped back and gazed lovingly into his eyes. "I am sorry to have to report to you that your sisters, Lynn and Nancy, have been taken into the Dark Kingdom."

A sharp pain pierced his heart. Nick felt his knees buckle beneath him, and he crumpled to the ground. Immediately, Bethany and Lazari were beside him. Lazari lowered his head and brushed his rider's shoulder with his velvet-soft lips. Bethany knelt down next to him and encircled him in her arms. Surprisingly, however, though he felt weak, Nick did not feel a sense of panic or fear. The warmth that Urijah had given him buoyed him up and gave him the capacity to speak calmly. "Tell me what has happened," he said, looking into the bright blue eyes of the Lord of Celestia from where he kneeled on the ground in front of the majestic unicorn.

"All I know at this point has come secondhand. I feel it would be best if we traveled to the Animal Kingdom and investigated the situation ourselves."

Lazari scooped up Nick and tossed him on his back. "Let us go immediately, my friend."

Nick nodded. His only desire, at this point, was to get to the bottom of this and find out just what had happened to his sisters. Lazari, reading his thoughts, set off at a canter to the edge of Celestia. Urijah, Helam, Mastis, and Bethany, astride Shema, followed close behind.

As they stepped out of the gardens of Celestia and into the Animal Kingdom, several animals of many species were gathered, awaiting their anticipated arrival. The mare that was Lazari's earthly mother stepped forward. Two cowering hyenas followed behind her, their heads bowed in shame.

"My dear Lazari," she began, placing her muzzle up to that of her son and blowing out warm air. She looked at Nick. "And you, Nicholas. It is wonderful to see you again."

"Thank you for being here to meet us, Mother," Lazari responded.

"Yes. I only wish it were under happier circumstances," answered the Hanoverian mare.

At that moment, Urijah stepped into the meadow that marked the beginning of the Animal Kingdom. Immediately, every animal, large and small, bent one front leg and lowered their heads into a respectful bow. All of the animals esteemed and revered the Lord of Celestia, and they felt it an honor to be in his presence. His visits to the Animal Kingdom were rare, and many of the animals had never seen the magnificent unicorn in person before this day. But they all knew of him and the great power of his love for every animal. Some of the animals kept their eyes downcast. Others looked up through their eyelashes to sneak a peek at the sparkling white unicorn. The two hyenas that stood behind Lazari's mother dropped their bellies to the ground and covered their heads with their front paws, ashamed to be seen by the great Urijah.

"Please arise, my friends," said Urijah kindly. "It is wonderful to be with you. I only wish it were under a happier state of affairs. Who is prepared to report on the events that have transpired this day?"

Lazari's mother stepped forward. "I will, my lord."

Urijah looked down at the lovely mare with a warm smile. "Proceed."

"As you know, Nancy and Lynn have been coming to the Animal Kingdom for quite some time."

Urijah nodded his head knowingly. "Please continue."

"They have won the hearts of all the animals with their soft, caressing hands and warm, cradling arms. Their sweet voices are like music to our ears." As the mare spoke, the animals who stood around her nodded in agreement. Some stood quietly weeping. "They were willing to help anywhere they were asked, but they were especially helpful with the new animals that came to us as infants." She sighed deeply as she thought of Nick's younger sisters.

The mare paused and turned her head and neck around to wipe a tear from her eye by rubbing her face on her shoulder. She shook her forelock out of her eyes before continuing. "Early yesterday morning these two scoundrels"—and she motioned with her head toward the two hyenas who still cowered on the ground behind her—"convinced our young friends to follow them under the pretense of helping to rescue some young pups from danger. They carried them to the edge of the Dark Kingdom, and there they . . ." Lazari's mother shuddered and took in a deep breath to compose herself, ". . . turned them over to Hasbadana." She said the name of the lord of the Dark Kingdom with disdain. Her eyes narrowed as she swished her tail and kicked back her hind leg, striking the shoulder of the nearest hyena. He jumped back with a yelp before quickly resuming his crouching position, and immediately hid his face under his front paws again.

Nick could feel his heart beating strongly in his chest. His hands clenched into tight fists as perspiration dripped from his forehead. He was having a hard time absorbing what he was hearing. It was too painful.

Urijah listened silently without any outward show of emotion. As the mare finished her story, he turned his attention away from her and glared at the two hyenas. His piercing blue eyes captured and held them. They looked up and met his gaze. Shame caused them to slink backward, but they were unable to take their eyes away from Urijah's stare. When Urijah spoke, it was with such power that even the wispy clouds in the sky melted away. "What do you have to say for yourselves?"

The closest hyena spoke first. "Oh, mighty and wonderful Lord Urijah, we come before you to beg your forgiveness. We fell victim to Hasbadana's deceit. He promised us great power and glory if we would help him."

"Help him do what?" roared Urijah.

The second hyena, quaking like an aspen leaf, spoke up with a stutter, "H-H-He said he just wanted to meet the h-humans. H-H-He . . . said he would not h-hurt them. He j-just wanted to t-talk with them."

"And you believed him?" said Urijah with skepticism, his eyes narrowing.

"Well, he promised!" insisted the first.

"Yes, he p-p-promised," echoed the second.

Urijah paced back and forth in front of the crouching hyenas. Nick watched him as he moved elegantly back and forth, his long, white tail swishing from side to side. The majestic Lord of Celestia stopped and looked down at the hyenas again. "Tell me, did Hasbadana come into the Animal Kingdom to take the girls?"

The two hyenas took turns responding.

"Oh, no. We never saw him. But we could hear his voice speaking sweetly to the humans."

"He k-k-kept asking them to come c-closer to the edge of the l-l-light. 'Come c-c-closer, come c-c-closer,' he kept saying."

"He said he wanted to be able to see and hear them better."

"J-J-Just as they were nearly touching the d-darkness, we heard a loud sucking noise and both girls were p-pulled into the D-Dark Kingdom."

"Once they disappeared, all we heard was a loud, vile-sounding laugh."

All of the animals listened with rapt attention, shock and sorrow written across their faces. Bethany grasped Nick's arm as he stood stiffly beside her. Nick slowly took his eyes off the despicable hyenas and looked back at Urijah, eager to receive some comfort from him and trusting that only he would be able to recommend a resolution to this painful predicament.

Urijah stopped pacing. He released the hyenas from his gripping gaze, raised his head, and looked up toward the sky. He stood silently, contemplating the situation for quite some time. No animal or human moved a muscle or made a sound.

After what seemed like a very long time, Urijah slowly lowered his head and turned to look at Nick and Bethany. His bright blue eyes were filled with compassion and love. His large iridescent horn sparkled and sent out little twinkling rainbows as he spoke. "Nicholas and Bethany, the responsibility must be yours to return to the Dark Kingdom to rescue your sisters. It is my hope that the love you, Nicholas, hold for your sisters will be sufficient to liberate them."

He paused and looked down, clearly conflicted with the assignment he was giving them. When he looked back at them, there were tears in his eyes. "My beloved friends, I cannot honestly say that you will be able to succeed. Hasbadana has become very powerful. I do not know to what extent he will be able to influence you. Nor do I know how he will respond to your great power."

He shook his head slowly from side to side. "No, I just do not know what awaits you. But I do know that you are the best chance that Lynn and Nancy have."

Nick stepped forward, his chin up, his jaw set firmly. "Of course, Urijah. It is up to me to save my sisters. But do you feel it is wise to send Bethany as well?"

"I hesitate only because I know how painful her last imprisonment in the Dark Kingdom was," said Urijah, as he turned to look at the beautiful young girl, her brown wavy hair falling softly around her face.

Bethany stepped forward. Her striking brown eyes sparkled. Her cheeks were flushed. Her dark pink lips were set in a straight line. When she spoke, she spoke with confidence, her chin lifted slightly. "I am not the same person that was once Hasbadana's prisoner. I am now a member of the Legion of the Unicorn. I will combine my power with Nicholas's. Together we will have a greater chance of succeeding than just he alone."

Urijah smiled. "So it shall be."

chapter 10

Return to the Dark Kingdom

Urijah turned toward the two hyenas, who remained in their cowering position, their shame causing them to wish a mountain would fall upon them and hide them from the piercing gaze of the majestic Lord of Celestia. When he spoke, Urijah's voice roared like thunder and pervaded the entire Animal Kingdom, causing all of the animals to throw up their heads and step back a stride. "You despicable creatures, you lowest of the lowlifes, you who dishonor the very name of animal!" With each insult, the hyenas pressed themselves tighter against the ground. Then his voice softened. "It will be necessary for you to repent of your evil deeds."

The two hyenas, sensing a particle of hope, lifted just their eyes to look at Urijah.

The Lord of Celestia looked down at them, his long, white forelock falling to one side of his horn. "I will be sending you to escort our unicorn riders to the exact spot where the young girls were taken into the Dark Kingdom."

The two hyenas responded together, "Oh, yes, Lord Urijah. We can do that! We will gladly do that."

Lazari and Shema, standing silently behind their riders, stepped forward until they stood abreast of Nick and Bethany. "Lord Urijah," said Lazari, "we desire to be of assistance."

"Of course you do. I expected nothing less. However, you realize that you cannot accompany your riders into the Dark Kingdom."

"Yes, we realize this. However, we can carry them swiftly to the edge of the light. That will help them preserve their energy."

"Very good," said Urijah with a nod of his splendid white head.

Nick and Bethany mounted their unicorns. The two hyenas arose from their crouching position, spun on their hind legs, and headed toward a large grove of trees on the far side of the meadow. Lazari and Shema stayed on their heels as the doglike creatures ran gracefully through the woods, their large shoulders and long front legs enabling them to take extended strides and cover ground quickly.

After traveling quite a distance, the group entered a lovely garden, the prettiest place Nick had ever seen outside of Celestia. Roses were growing in cultivated squares surrounded by neatly trimmed boxwood hedges. Each square was home to a different color of rose, and every color was represented, from white to black and every color in between.

"I know this place," said Bethany with excitement in her voice.

"You do?" responded Nick as he looked over at her with an expression of surprise.

"Oh yes, but I have never seen it from this side before."

"What do you mean?" Nick asked as both unicorns slowed to a walk.

"I used to gaze at this garden from the Dark Kingdom." She motioned with her hand toward the far side of the rose garden to where a tall hedge of roses provided a barrier between the two kingdoms. "Behind that wall of roses is the Dark Kingdom. When Hasbadana first captured me, he allowed me to roam the Dark Kingdom. I spent most of my time in what I named the 'Forlorn Forest.' It is just on the other side of that hedge." She looked down and her cheeks flushed a bright pink as she softly added, "I watered many of the trees with my tears as I gazed through the hedge into this garden."

Nick reached over the narrow space that separated the two unicorns and grasped her hand. Giving it a squeeze, he smiled and said, "And now you are here."

She looked up at him and smiled warmly. "Yes, now I am here."

The hyenas led them through the square rose beds and up to a section of the hedge where an arched trellis supported a climbing rosebush. The roses on this bush were unique. They twinkled and changed colors as though they were one of the flowers growing in Celestia. From this close proximity to the hedge, Nick was able to examine the plants more carefully. On the side facing the Animal Kingdom, the hedge was covered with shiny green leaves and full aromatic roses. But on the back side of the hedge were no leaves or roses, only large, sharp thorns. Nick's body shook in an involuntary shiver as he looked at the foreboding thorns.

The two hyenas stopped and looked back at the unicorns and their riders. "This is where the two girl humans were pulled into the Dark Kingdom," said one of them.

"Th-They w-w-went through that t-t-trellis," added the other.

Nick slid off Lazari and stood beside his unicorn. *Can we do this?* he asked Lazari in his thoughts.

You must, and so you will, responded Lazari as he turned his beautiful head and encircled Nick with his dark bay neck. Nick interlocked the fingers of his right hand in the silky black mane and with his left hand, stroked his unicorn's face. He ran his fingertips up and down the glistening amber horn that adorned the center of Lazari's forehead.

Bethany dismounted gracefully, hugged Shema's neck, and stepped in front of Nick. Reaching out to take his hand, she said, "It is time to go. Lynn and Nancy need us."

Without looking back, Nick and Bethany stepped through the rose-covered trellis, leaving the light behind.

****

Stepping from the light to the dark was like traveling through time and space to another world. All of Nick's senses were keenly aware of the changes around them. The beautiful music that always permeated Celestia and floated across the Animal Kingdom was missing. The silence that replaced it was deafening. Their ears ached as they searched for some kind of sound to grasp on to. Unlike the last time Nick was here when the wind seemed to be blowing from all directions at once, this time everything was absolutely still. Even their breath, as it left their bodies, seemed to stop in midstream as if afraid to enter this foreign space. The sun hung in the sky as a dull white orb. Its light and warmth were unable to penetrate the darkness that covered the kingdom. The only usable light was that which emanated from Nick and Bethany's bodies, but even that could not reach very far.

As Bethany had warned, when they entered the Dark Kingdom they stepped into the area she had named the "Forlorn Forest." All of the trees were bare skeletons, some black, some gray. Their branches reached up like fingers trying to grasp some sustenance from the ice-cold sun. Nothing was forthcoming. Yet hope had not abandoned them as they continued to force their leafless branches upward.

Unlike the trees in Celestia that would graciously move out of their way to let them pass, these trees seemed bent on thwarting their progress. Gray and black branches intertwined and formed a tangled, web-like barrier in whichever direction they stepped. The two unicorn riders commanded the branches to part and let them through. But the trees did not obey. Nick and Bethany searched unsuccessfully for an unencumbered path to follow. With resolve, they realized they needed to create their own path. At times they were forced to crawl under the branches, sliding like snakes across the rocky ground. Other times they climbed over or through the branches.

After several hours of struggling and disentangling themselves and their clothing from the grasp of the sharp branches, they emerged from the unfriendly forest, covered with rips and scratches. The thick, silver fluid that had replaced their blood when they were made immortal oozed out through several tears in their skin. Bethany set to work healing both of them while Nick commanded their clothing to mend itself.

Once the repairs to clothing and bodies were complete, Nick looked toward the area they had just entered. Before them, and as far as the eye could see, was a barren wasteland. The surface of the ground was cracked and dry. Lines marred the surface, reminiscent of the way skin cells look under a microscope. The landscape was virtually flat, broken only by the occasional outcropping of jagged rocks. The entire area was a medium gray in color with no variation in shades. The light cast from their bodies found nothing to reflect off of in the sand and clay surface of the ground. All was dull.

The sun continually changed its orientation so it was impossible to tell which direction they were headed. Up to this point, Nick had relied completely on Bethany to lead them. He turned to her once again. "Which way should we go now?"

She looked up at him, the strain of returning to this awful place now evident in her eyes. Yet her mouth was set in a firm, determined line. "I call this place the 'Desert of Despair.' We must cross this barren land, but it will take us several hours to do so." She leaned down and attempted to call forth water from the ground, but nothing happened. She tried again and again, but the parched ground would not obey her.

Nick tried and failed as well. "That's strange," he said after his third failed attempt. "I was able to command the elements when we came to the Dark Kingdom the first time. For some reason, this time neither the trees nor the ground obey us."

"Well, let's get moving. We can get water from the lake," said Bethany. Before Nick could respond, she set out across the Desert of Despair. Nick followed a few steps behind, marveling that she seemed confident in her ability to lead him to his sisters.

After walking in silence for what must have been several miles, Nick spoke. "Bethany?"

"Yes?"

"How do you know where Lynn and Nancy will be?"

"Because I know Hasbadana. He will have taken them to his castle. It is the only place he likes to be. He hardly ever leaves, preferring to send his henchmen to do his bidding," she said, speaking as though it hurt to even discuss Hasbadana.

"And you are sure we are going in the right direction?"

"Positive."

Confidence in Bethany's knowledge of the Dark Kingdom replaced Nick's concern, and he walked behind her in rhythm with her steps, silent once again.

As they walked, they detected no sign of life around them. They seemed to be all alone. The emptiness began to work its way under Nick's skin, and he found himself looking back and forth, searching the darkness for any sort of observer. "Do you think Hasbadana knows we are here?"

"He absolutely knows we are here," Bethany responded confidently.

"How can you be so sure? I haven't seen any sign of his dark unicorns, nor has there been any indication that we are being followed."

Bethany continued to walk with a long, determined stride even as she answered. "He can feel your power and it causes him pain."

"Pain?" asked Nick in both bewilderment and disbelief.

"Yes, pain. The minute we stepped through the trellis, the light and love we brought with us pierced him like sharp needles. The closer we get, the more the pain intensifies. That is why he will be so desperate to draw your power from you. It is the only way he can stop hurting. The power you have developed is so much greater now that you are a member of the Legion of the Unicorn than it was when you were a mere immortal human and confronted him before. The pain must be driving him mad."

"And don't forget to double it. You are not the same person he once held captive, either."

She chuckled. "That's true. It almost, but not quite, makes me feel sorry for him."

The hours of hiking across the dismal, gray, and cracked desert passed slowly. Nothing in the landscape captured his interest, so Nick just trudged along, following the footprints that Bethany left behind in the dusty ground.

At last, Bethany stopped and pointed. "There it is. There is the lake."

"Don't tell me, let me guess. You named it 'Lonesome Lake.'"

Bethany turned and flashed him a smile. "Close. I call it Loveless Lake."

"That's appropriate as well," Nick responded, smiling grimly.

"Hasbadana's castle is on the far shore." She looked forward and Nick followed her gaze. Loveless Lake was huge. Wispy patches of fog obscured the far shore, making it impossible to see the castle. They walked forward until they stood at the edge of the black water. Bethany bent down and scooped some cold water from the lake into her mouth. She looked up at Nick. "It doesn't taste great but it's wet, and since you're immortal, it can't kill you," she said with a laugh.

"Do we walk around the shoreline?" asked Nick.

"No. We will row."

Nick looked at her incredulously. But before he could verbalize his doubts, he caught a movement out of the corner of his eye. He turned and his mouth dropped as he watched a little rowboat slide silently across the still water, straight toward them.

"The only gift Hasbadana ever gave me," Bethany said with a sneer as she stepped from the shore into the front seat of the tiny rowboat.

Nick took his place at the oars. He took ahold of the handles of each paddle and dipped them into the water. Instantly, the boat began gliding forward, heading for the opposite shore. Every so often, as though he felt obligated, Nick broke the surface of the water with his oars. But the boat was not waiting for him nor dependent upon him as it carried them across Loveless Lake. Silently, the boat skimmed across the black water, moving seemingly from its own power source. The boat was the only thing that seemed to disturb the surface of the water. Elsewhere, for as far out as they could see, the lake was perfectly smooth and still. However, like a frozen river, the currents ran strong beneath the surface.

Bethany sat in the front of the boat, leaning over one side. She silently, pensively gazed at her reflection in the black, glass-like surface of the water, still amazed at the beauty she saw there. Her reflection revealed the warm glow that emanated from her lovely round face—a glow that stood in sharp contrast to the darkness around her.

Suddenly, her face disappeared in a ripple of water and was replaced with the ghostly, pallid image of a unicorn appearing beneath the surface of the water, its red eyes glaring at her. She jerked back with a gasp, her hands clutching her throat.

"What is it, Bethany?" said Nick with concern.

"I-I'm not sure . . . perhaps I was just imagining it . . . but I thought I saw a unicorn under the water."

Nick looked over the side of the boat. He saw nothing but the smooth black surface of the water. If the apparition had been there, it was gone now. "Come sit by me," he said, patting the wooden bench on which he sat.

Without hesitation, Bethany scooted back in the boat and sat beside Nick. He dropped both oars and put one arm around her, pulling her tightly against him. He could feel her thin body shiver though there was no sensation of cold in the air. Stillness and silence surrounded them on all sides.

"Everything will be okay, Bethany. As Lazari is always reminding me, we have been given the power of love. There is no power in fear."

She nodded silently even as her eyes gazed all around them, searching for what, she knew not.

Up ahead, the fog grew more dense as it sat on top of the lake. But above the fog, the outline of a castle was visible, its windows glowing with a pale yellow light, the only light they had seen in the Dark Kingdom.

"Hasbadana's castle," said Bethany as she pressed her body closer to Nick. "The power of love, not fear," she whispered to herself.

Nick wrapped his arm tighter around her shoulder in an attempt to comfort her. He was keenly aware of how difficult this must be for her.

The castle disappeared from view as the boat carried them silently into the thick fog.

chapter 11

valhalla

The boat came to a sudden stop as the bow rammed into an old, rotting wooden dock. The light from Nick and Bethany's bodies revealed a rocky shoreline just beyond the dock and a narrow path that disappeared into the fog silently awaiting visitors. Nick and Bethany climbed out of their little boat and onto the rickety wooden pier. It creaked and groaned under their weight and shook as they moved from one post rail to the next. They carefully worked their way the short distance to the land. Both were grateful to place their feet on solid ground once they reached the end of the dock.

Bethany led the way up the narrow path as it meandered deeper into the fog. The fog seemed to be getting more dense with each step they took. As they walked, they could only see a few feet in front of them.

Nick kept thinking about how much he admired Bethany's courage. He knew this was not easy for her. In reality, he was underestimating the terror raging in her heart. He had no idea how much energy she was expending trying to suppress her fear.

Slowly, the image of a castle materialized through the fog. The structure seemed to arise from the ground and stand as a ghastly formation silhouetted against the even darker sky. As they drew closer, the architectural details stood out more clearly. The rough-hewn stones were poorly fitted together, leaving gaps between them. The metal around the windows and the hinges on the doors was corroded with rust. The beams and door planks were rotting from the outside in. Only the pale yellow glow at the windows, emanating from a source of light on the inside, offered a hint of welcome from the structure.

Several uneven steps led up to the main entrance, which was covered with a large wooden plank door. Nick and Bethany climbed the steps. Even as Nick raised his hand to knock on the crumbling wood, the door opened. The silver talismans that hung around the necks of the two unicorn riders had become increasingly warm the closer they got to Hasbadana's castle. Now they were too hot to touch, an unnecessary warning of danger.

"Welcome to Valhalla," said Hasbadana in an artificially jovial voice. The lord of the Dark Kingdom stood in the center of the antechamber. He was standing squarely on all four hooves, his enormous head held high; his bright red eyes locked on them.

Nick and Bethany stepped into the foyer of the castle. The door swung shut behind them with a bang, sending splinters of wood clattering to the floor. Both guests jumped at the loud sound, their ears having adjusted themselves to a world of silence.

As soon as Nick could feel his nerves relax a little, he looked around at their surroundings. The round room was dimly lit by a few burning torches secured to the stone walls. Dark shadows cast black lines across the floor and over the giant unicorn that stood in the center of the room.

"So, my young human friends, you have come at last. I should ask what kept you, but I'm confident you were preoccupied with the heroic tasks you are assigned to perform." He chuckled deep in his throat, as did several other dark unicorns barely visible in the shadows around the edge of the circular chamber.

Nick and Bethany cast their eyes round about them. They counted a dozen other dark unicorns who appeared to be standing guard.

"You know why we are here. We have come to retrieve my sisters. We will do so now and be on our way," said Nick calmly yet with boldness.

Hasbadana let out a deep, long whinny and shook his big head, his long forelock flopping from one side of his horn to the other. "Why be in such a rush? Whatever could be the motivation for traveling so very far and not taking time to enjoy the destination?" he said with a sardonic smile.

He stepped forward. "Before you depart, let me show you around my lovely home. I call this castle 'Valhalla,' the true destination of the worthy dead. You will notice that I have adopted some of the architectural features of Urijah's own castle." He motioned with his head to the columns that supported the circular dome under which he stood. "You will please appreciate the columns that support this dome. Rather than the ten unicorn virtues, I have simplified down to five. Each column represents what I have labeled my 'Five Pillars of the Dark Kingdom.' The first is Doubt. The second is Discouragement. The third is Despair. The fourth is Deceit. And the final and most powerful pillar is Domination. These are the virtues that have made me what I am: the most powerful force in heaven and earth." He finished with his voice rising in a crescendo.

Nick and Bethany stood silently, fighting back the feeling of fear trying to strip them of their power. Nick looked around at the carved columns depicting unicorns in battle. In every scene that worked its way around the columns, Hasbadana was depicted as the victor over man and beast. Above them, the pillars supported a dome, reminiscent of the dome in the council chambers in Celestia. But this dome, rather than sending down a shower of colored stars, was filled with a swirling black mist.

On the cold stone floor between each column stood two or three dark unicorns, a look of menace on their faces. A few were pawing their front hooves in apparent impatience to be rid of the niceties being forced upon the situation by their leader. The entire panorama in which they now stood could easily have been a Francisco de Goya painting, the Spanish artist who, in his latter life, filled his paintings with gore and darkness.

Apparently, Hasbadana had also depleted his supply of patience. He lowered his head and narrowed his red eyes. "Now, let us get to the business at hand, shall we? So, you actually believe you are capable of challenging the lord of the Dark Kingdom and leaving as the victor?" he said with a sneer.

"We have not come to battle. We have come to appeal to you to release Lynn and Nancy in a nonconfrontational manner," said Nick, raising his chin to look directly into Hasbadana's flaming red eyes. For a moment, his gaze was locked on the evil unicorn's eyes, held there by Hasbadana himself. Nick reached up with his hand and grasped the talisman glowing brightly as it hung around his neck. It took a great deal of self-control to break away from Hasbadana's hold.

The lord of the Dark Kingdom, respecting Nick's strength for perhaps the first time, smiled. "I desire nothing less. I detest violence after all." The unicorns around them nickered softly.

"But I am afraid I cannot simply release my prisoners. They belong to me now, as I'm sure you can understand."

Fighting the anger swelling up in his breast, Nick swallowed hard before he responded. "I do *not* understand for they do *not* belong to you any more than any of these dark unicorns belong to you," he said as he made a sweeping motion with his arm, hoping to gain the support of even some of Hasbadana's followers. The dark unicorns looked up in surprise at the audaciousness of this human. A few, however, liked the sound of what he was saying even while doubting its validity.

A low growling sound, uncharacteristic of horses or unicorns, arose from deep within the giant creature. "So, you think I do not have the right to possess the young female humans? Well, perhaps you would like to see them for yourselves, hum?"

"Yes, I would," answered Nick boldly.

"Then follow me," said Hasbadana as he turned on his haunches and walked toward the far end of the antechamber. Nick and Bethany followed him, and the twelve dark unicorn guards fell in, two by two, behind them. Nick and Bethany each glanced over their shoulders at their escorts before turning their attention forward once more.

Hasbadana led them down a long, dark hallway, lit by an occasional flaming torch. Nick noticed that the walls of the hallway showed signs of the same amount of deterioration evident on the outside of the castle. The twisting flames on the torches caused their bodies to cast eerie shadows that bounced and wiggled along the jagged walls, looking like monsters from a childhood nightmare.

The floor was made of rough, irregular stones just like the walls. Unlike the silence of the hoof steps of the unicorns in Celestia, these unicorns' hooves clanged loudly on the stone floor. Nick and Bethany occasionally stumbled over the uneven stones as they walked along in the dimly lit passageway.

Nick remembered seeing this hallway, or one like it, through Bethany's thoughts when she was held captive in this very castle. He glanced over at her. She was walking quickly to keep up but with her jaw firmly set in a look of determination. Nick wondered, again, if it had been wise to bring her here and put her through this. He was well aware that she had been invaluable as a guide, but perhaps it had been cruel of him to bring her this far. Maybe it would have been wiser to send her back once they had reached Loveless Lake. His mind searched for her thoughts but found only a black barrier. One of the skills that Bethany had developed was that talent also possessed by Portlas. As a defense mechanism, she could block her thoughts from interception by others.

A few passageways jutted off from this main corridor down which the dark unicorns were walking and the unicorn riders were stumbling. It was down one of these that Hasbadana finally turned. Several doors sat tightly closed within stone archways that had been built into the walls. Hasbadana passed all of them as he headed for the door at the end of the corridor. Just as he reached the door, it opened of its own accord to let him enter, scraping noisily on the uneven stone floor. The dark lord stopped and turned his head back to face them. "Here we are. This is their new home. I am sure you will be impressed. I spared no effort to ensure their comfort." He smiled, turned back, and entered the room with Nick and Bethany rushing in behind him.

Hasbadana stopped just inside the room, and Nick and Bethany ran past him before they came to a sudden stop. Initially, as their eyes adjusted to the darkened room, all Nick could see were two black swirling cones of mist. Then Nick gasped. Hanging suspended in the center of the swirling cones of mist were his young sisters, Lynn in one cone, Nancy in the other. Their heads hung down with their hair falling over their faces. Their bodies appeared to be limp, as they slowly revolved with the movement of the mist.

Nick felt his chest fill with pain as the love within him, the source of his power, battled with the anger and, yes, hate that struggled to conquer him. Nick turned on Hasbadana, his fists finding the beast's neck. "What have you done to them?" he yelled as he pounded on the dark unicorn.

Hasbadana reared up as he let out a scornful laugh. "I thought you desired 'nonconfrontation.' Where, oh where, are those wonderful unicorn virtues of patience and love when you most need them?" He laughed.

Bethany ran to Nick and pulled him back. Two of Hasbadana's guards pushed both of them back against the rough stone walls and held them at bay with their sharp horns pressed against Nick and Bethany's bodies.

Bethany kept her arms wrapped tightly around Nick even as he glared at Hasbadana. "Our power comes from love," she whispered in his ear.

Using all of his strength, he drew upon the love he felt for his sisters. When he finally spoke, it was with calmness and control. "Release them, Hasbadana. They are of no use to you."

"On the contrary, my dear boy. They have been very useful. In point of fact, they have already served their purpose. They have enticed you to come here. That was my sole objective in bringing them to my lovely abode."

"Then you no longer need them. I am here. You can release them."

"A tantalizing idea, to be sure," said Hasbadana as he walked in a circle around the two spirals of mist that held the girls captive. "Yes, indeed, a very tantalizing idea. Let me contemplate this for a moment." He paused and smiled. "Agreed! I will exchange their freedom for yours."

"You must release Lynn, Nancy, and Bethany."

"Three for one? That hardly seems just."

"That is the deal."

"Somehow I don't feel that you are really in a very good bargaining position." He laughed and his guards joined with him, stopping when he did. "All right, then. Three for one but just so that my followers can see what a magnanimous leader I truly am. 'Magnanimous' is a term I frequently, and with great justification, use to describe myself." He looked around at his guards and they all nodded their agreement. Some murmured words of concurrence.

He turned back to look at Nick, who was still being restrained by both Bethany and the two guards. "Perhaps Nicholas, the great unicorn rider," he added with a tone of mockery in his voice, "would like to be the one to release his sisters." A sardonic smile once again crossed his face.

Nick stepped forward.

"Ah, I suspected as much. Always the hero," said Hasbadana with a sneer. "You need only touch the mist of darkness with your *love*, and it will dissolve under your great power."

Nick turned his back to Hasbadana and walked toward one of the spiraling cones, his hand outstretched. Just as he was about to touch the mist he heard Bethany scream, "Nicholas, no!"

Too late, he turned to see Hasbadana blowing a stream of black smoke from his nostrils directly toward him. The stream encircled his body, and he was immediately caught up in a swirling cone of mist of his own. Before he even realized what had happened he was overcome by cold. The room within the castle of Valhalla disappeared from his consciousness.

Chapter 12

The Savior

Light and warmth replaced the darkness that had held Nick prisoner for so long. He awoke to find himself lying on the floor of a stone room.

Where am I? he asked himself. Slowly the fog cleared from his mind. He remembered coming to Hasbadana's castle of Valhalla and finding Lynn and Nancy in their prisons of mist. From that point to this awakening, however, he had no memory—only a sensation of cold and dark. He realized he was staring up at the ceiling above him, which was brightly lit. He turned his head toward the source of the light. Standing to his side was Urijah.

"Urijah," he said with excitement, joy filling his body and causing tears to well up in his eyes. "What are you . . . ?" He stopped in midsentence as understanding filled his heart with dread. "You came for us?"

Urijah nodded his big, white head. The magnificent Lord of Celestia stood proudly beside him, looking down at him with nothing but love in his eyes.

"But the unicorns are not allowed to come to the Dark Kingdom. How did you get here?"

"We have always had the power to come if we so chose. It is just that, under all other circumstances, we have been commanded not to subject ourselves to the absence of love. I chose to come to save you."

Suddenly, Nick remembered his own purpose in coming. He sat up with a start and looked frantically around him. There, beside him on the floor, just recovering from their own stupors, were Bethany, Lynn, and Nancy. Looking around the room, Nick found no sign of the mysterious black cones of mist that had held them captive. Relieved to see all of them safe, Nick turned his attention back to Urijah. It was only then that he noticed the rusted black chains around the Lord of Celestia's sparkling white neck. The large metal shackles dropped down both shoulders and wrapped themselves around his legs. More restraints were connected to each of his strong legs, acting as hobbles.

"Urijah! You are bound," Nick exclaimed with shock.

At this, Hasbadana stepped forward from where he had been standing in the shadows. "Yes. He belongs to me now," he said with a derisive smile.

"No! You can't do that!"

"It appears that I already have, now doesn't it?" responded Hasbadana as he walked slowly around Urijah, looking at him as one would any prize catch.

Nick jumped to his feet. "Urijah, you have the power to free yourself. Do it! Do it now," yelled Nick, panic filling his entire being.

Softly and calmly, Urijah smiled at Nick, sparkling rainbows dancing around his horn. "While it is true that I have the power, I cannot use it. I have given my word, and my word is my true bond."

"What word? What did you say?"

"I have come to trade myself for you."

Nick dropped to his knees as the full realization of what had transpired in his behalf weighed down upon him. "Oh, Urijah," he whispered. "Why?"

"There is no greater love than this, my son," said Urijah softly.

By this time, the three young women had fully recovered and were listening to what was being said. Each rose to their knees, hands clasped, heads bowed, and tears flowing freely.

A sudden feeling of anger filled Nick, and he jerked his head up and glared at Hasbadana. "Hasbadana! You can't do this," he shouted, shaking the walls and sending tiny pebbles rattling to the floor.

Urijah took half a step forward, but the chains that wrapped around his legs constrained him. "Nicholas, this is as it should be. Do not let anger deprive you of your power. Do not be sad for me. I have done this willingly. All will be well."

Nick scrambled to his feet and instantly crossed the short distance that separated him from his savior. He threw his arms around Urijah's strong, white neck and pressed his face into the stallion's flowing mane. He let the tears flow freely. Sobbing violently, he choked out, "This can't be the only way. There must be something else we can do. I am not worth your sacrifice."

Urijah pulled back so he could look Nick in the eyes. "Oh, but you are. Do not ever think that, or my sacrifice would be in vain."

Hasbadana stepped up and pushed Nick back with his cold, black horn, causing Nick to stumble and fall backward. Bethany leapt to her feet and caught him. Hasbadana turned so he was facing the four humans. "Enough! I have endured enough. The agreement has been made. Now leave before I change my mind," he shouted.

Lynn and Nancy stood up and stepped forward until they were beside Nick and Bethany. All four turned and looked at Urijah. The beautiful white unicorn sparkled, filling the room with light and warmth, something that pained Hasbadana and contributed to his ill mood.

Urijah looked at them and, with a smile on his face, nodded his head. Without saying another word, the magnificent Lord of Celestia looked down and closed his eyes.

Huddled tightly together, Nick, Bethany, and Nick's sisters were pushed and prodded out of the room and down the hall by several of Hasbadana's dark unicorns. An evil laugh, an agony-filled whinny, and the slam of a heavy wooden door bid them farewell.

The four humans clung to each other, the three young women in front, Nick in the back, attempting to act as a shield from the sharp pokes that the dark unicorns' horns were inflicting. Bethany, Lynn, and Nancy were weeping openly, looking down at the ground as they shuffled along. Nick, on the other hand, was looking all around, carefully memorizing every detail of Hasbadana's castle as they passed through. Idea after idea on how to liberate Urijah sprouted in his brain, only to be quickly weeded out. Sneaking back into Valhalla to rescue him on their own would not work any better than storming the castle with an army. Urijah would never come. Certainly he had the power on his own to overcome his imprisonment, but he had freely given himself, and he would never go back on his word. *Sometimes those unicorn virtues can really get in the way*, thought Nick.

By the time they reached the large antechamber and found themselves standing beneath the mist of darkness swirling around the high dome above them, Nick still had no idea what he should do.

It was Hasbadana's five pillars that suddenly provided inspiration. Nick had not paid much attention when Hasbadana had first recited his version of the unicorn virtues: Doubt, Discouragement, Despair, Deceit, and Domination. Nick looked around him at the five pillars, carefully contemplating each one. It was easy to see how Hasbadana had worked his way to the final destination of Domination. But what had started him on this path in the first place?

"Doubt? Doubt about what?" he wondered aloud.

His three companions looked back at him.

"What did you say?" asked Lynn.

Still looking around at the five pillars, he replied over his shoulder. "What does Hasbadana doubt?"

Suddenly he knew the answer and he turned around quickly, light and excitement in his eyes and written on his face. "What does Hasbadana doubt?" he repeated with increasing animation.

The girls looked at each other and shook their heads, not understanding what he was getting at.

"What does Hasbadana doubt?" he asked a third time, even louder this time.

"I don't know," said Lynn.

Bethany narrowed her eyes and cocked her head. "Himself," she said in a whisper.

"Exactly!" said Nick with enthusiasm. "He doubts himself. That is what started him on this evil path in the first place. Look around you at these pillars." The young unicorn rider walked around the circle of columns, pointing to each one as he named them. "Doubt, Discouragement, Despair, Deceit, and Domination." He stopped moving and looked at the girls. "Yet each one is carved with depictions of Hasbadana himself being the victor. Step by step, this is how he got to where he is. He is fighting his own doubts, his own discouragement, and his own despair. Eventually, he decided that while he could not rid himself of those emotions, the only way to triumph over them was to use deceit and domination."

Pacing back and forth now as the young women watched and wondered where he was going with this, he continued. "We need to heal Hasbadana of the doubt that set him on this path in the first place." Looking up into their surprised faces, he said again, "We need to *heal* Hasbadana!"

"Heal Hasbadana?" each girl said softly, contemplating the implications and seemingly impossibility of such an idea.

Each of the dark unicorns escorting them out of Valhalla let out nickers of amusement. "Good luck with that one," said one as they pushed them forward toward the rotting wooden doors. The doors opened for them and they stepped out onto the sloping stone steps.

Suddenly, their descent was interrupted by the sound of Hasbadana's loud, booming voice. "Farewell, my friends." The evil lord's laugher shook the ground around them.

Nick and the young women turned in unison to see the giant beast standing in the doorway of his castle, his Valhalla.

"Oh, and I want to mention one more thing. Nicholas, the great unicorn rider, I have changed the rules a bit. As you journeyed to my home, you may have noticed that you can no longer control the elements in my kingdom. I am so sorry to disappoint you, but I have found it necessary to prevent you from using your powers against me and mine." He neighed loudly as he stomped his feet before he grew silent once again. "I hope that will not cause you any inconvenience." He laughed, and his guards joined him as if on cue.

Instantly, Nick could hear Urijah's voice in his head. *You still have the power to provide protection for yourselves. Hasbadana cannot take that away from you.*

Urijah, we will be back! responded Nick through his thoughts.

Farewell, my son, were the last words Urijah sent before the heavy wooden doors slammed shut and splinters of wood rattled down onto the stone steps.

Chapter 13

Loveless Lake

As they walked down the narrow, winding path to the lake, Nick was lost deep in his own thoughts. He realized he had no idea how long he had been enveloped by the cone of black mist. He wondered how many days it had been since he had crossed this lake to face Hasbadana. He laughed at his own naiveté. How had he believed that he could just walk into Hasbadana's kingdom and convince the evil lord of the Dark Kingdom to let him take Lynn and Nancy home? Now Urijah was paying the price. He shook his head to clear it of the pain these thoughts caused. What could he have done differently? What *should* he have done differently? He forced himself to remember that Urijah had allowed, even *encouraged* him, to go on this mission. Then something that Urijah had said came to his mind: "My beloved friends, I cannot honestly say that you will be able to succeed." How much had Urijah foreseen? Had he known all along that Nick and Bethany would fail? Had he known he would have to trade his life for theirs even as he sent them off?

By this time, they reached the shore of Loveless Lake. Awaiting their return, the little rowboat bounced against the rotting pier, just where they had left it. The surface of Loveless Lake was not the quiet, black mirror it had been upon their arrival. Waves rolled in from the center of the lake and crashed against the pilings of the pier, causing it to creak with complaint. No fog sat softly on the surface of the water today, but that did not make visibility any better. Looking out across the lake, the black sky melted into the rolling black water. The line of separation could not be distinguished from where they stood looking out.

"We're crossing in that?" said Nancy, fear evident in her voice.

Bethany and Nick nodded solemnly.

"Okay, then," she said, drawing on her reserve of courage and turning to lead the way down to the dock.

Nick smiled as he watched her walk with determination out onto the shaking pier. He was reminded of one of her favorite sayings when they had lived on the earth. Whenever they were faced with a challenge and someone wanted to complain or, worse, give up, she would say: "Just pull up your big-girl pants!" Nancy had pulled up her big-girl pants and was heading out into the darkness.

Nancy stepped cautiously into the rocking boat, steadying herself by grabbing tightly to the sides. Once she had both feet firmly planted in the bottom of the boat, she turned and offered a hand of assistance to her family and friend while clutching tightly to the side of the boat with the other.

They all felt great relief once they were each seated on a wooden bench inside the tiny wooden boat. The girls gripped the edge of the boat firmly with their hands, staring into the darkness ahead of them. Nick took the oars and dipped them into the water. As before, the boat instantly lurched forward, heading for the opposite shore under its own power.

The waves that rolled violently across the lake brought the front of the little boat up and then dropped out from under it. The bow slammed down onto the surface of the lake and sent a spray of water over them. In just a few minutes, all four passengers were soaking wet. Pushing up, crashing down, wave after wave beat against them. But the boat continued to make progress across the violent waters. The wind blew from all directions at once, but their wet, immortal bodies were not affected by the severe cold. They held on tightly and focused their eyes straight ahead of them, searching for any sign of the far shore. No one said a word.

They eventually reached the center of the lake. Nick looked behind them and could no longer see the faint light from Valhalla's windows. Looking forward, he still could not see any evidence of a shoreline. It was as though they were being tossed around in the middle of a wet, black nothingness. He took a deep breath and called upon the love within him to fill the boat with a feeling of tranquility. Sensing the change immediately, Bethany turned in her position on the bench beside him and smiled. "Thank you," she said. "That helps."

Nick tried his powers on the water, attempting to calm them. He found, with great disappointment, that the father of lies had told the truth this time. The elements would not obey him. But he remembered that Urijah had promised they would be able to protect themselves, and he clung to that promise.

Without any warning, a crashing sound issued from the front of the boat and a pallid white horn pierced through the bottom of the craft. Lynn and Nancy screamed and fell back onto Nick and Bethany. The horn stayed in place and the boat began to spin. From all sides, more ashen, colorless unicorns reared up out of the water, their bodies lit by the light radiating from the four humans. The only color on their bodies was the red in their eyes. Some pawed the air and emitted a gurgling whinny. Others pitched their bodies forward, crashing into the boat. The rowboat tipped violently as it spun, first one way, then the other as the four passengers clung to each other. With shrill, ear-splitting screams, the pallid unicorns beat against the boat, dismantling it piece by piece.

The serenity that Nick had infused upon them could not have been more perfectly timed. His mind was clear and calm as he formulated a plan. Just as the sides of the boat were pulled apart, he sent a shield of energy around the four of them, forming a protective and buoyant bubble. The wooden seat they had been sitting upon sank into the black depths of the lake. But they remained on top of the water, floating in a protective iridescent ball of sparkling energy.

For a moment, all of the ghostly unicorns stopped their attack. They sank out of sight beneath the rough surface of Loveless Lake. For that same moment, Nick, Bethany, Lynn, and Nancy bounced from the top of one wave to another in silence . . . but only for a moment. With a rush, what must have been a dozen unicorns broke through the surface of the water and charged toward them from all sides. Others came up right beneath them. The force of the moving water sent the bubble high into the air. When they came down, the sharp horns were waiting for them.

Lynn and Nancy screamed in fear, but Bethany and Nick remained quiet and calm, confident in the promise they had been given by Urijah. As their iridescent shield touched down on the first sharp horn, it bent into a slightly concave shape before the unicorn jerked back in agony. Unicorn after unicorn attempted to burst through the bubble. One by one, the unicorns dove back into the water to avoid any further painful contact with the strange shelter.

As their floating shield dropped back down on top of the water, it resumed its perfectly round shape, having been poked and prodded with no resulting damage. As the last unicorn disappeared into the depths of Loveless Lake, the wind ceased blowing and the surface of the lake became perfectly smooth once again. The bubble that was protecting the four humans settled down into the water and stopped. The light from their bodies filled the bubble and it glowed from within. Beyond the sides of the lighted ball was darkness.

Nick and the young women looked at each other. Lynn spoke first. "Well, that was *interesting*. But now what do we do? We are sitting here, in the dark, on a lake inhabited by ghosts of unicorns, or whatever they are, in a bubble that isn't going anywhere."

Nick chuckled. "I'd say that's a pretty fair description of our situation, wouldn't you, Bethany?" he said, turning to Bethany who sat beside him, her legs extending up the sides of the bubble.

"Fair enough," she answered with a smile.

"How do we get out of here?" asked Nancy, perfectly confident that her brother, "the great unicorn rider," as Hasbadana had called him, would have a solution.

"We'll walk, of course," he said with enthusiasm. His response was greeted with three looks of disparagement.

"No, really! Do you remember that hamster you once owned, Lynn? Do you remember how you would put him in that clear, plastic exercise ball so he could run around without getting lost, and he would roll all around the house in it?"

"Uh, yes. Don't remind me. I've had to answer to that hamster in the Animal Kingdom!"

Nick laughed. "I'm sure you have! Let's all stand up and start walking. We just need Bethany to tell us which way to go."

"Well, let's give it a try," said Bethany as she struggled to her feet.

Bethany quickly discovered that standing was not an easy task, reminiscent of trying to stand on an air mattress or waterbed. By using the hands and heads of her companions, she finally managed to stand on her feet. Carefully, and with much grunting and groaning and a few failed attempts, she pulled the others up to join her. For a few moments they held onto one another, trying desperately to keep their balance. Once they were in a steady position Bethany looked around, thoughtfully considering their position.

"It's that way," she said, letting go of the others with one hand and pointing behind her.

"Oh, great," mumbled Lynn.

Slowly the band of stranded travelers shuffled around until they had arranged themselves in a straight line across the bubble with arms interlocked, facing the direction Bethany had pointed.

Nick was on one end, and all three female faces turned in unison to look at him. "Okay, we have to do this together. Everyone lift your right foot," he said. Four right feet lifted into the air about knee height while the left legs all wiggled as the four stranded travelers struggled to keep their balance. "Step!" All four right feet came down in front of the line of bodies, and the bubble rolled forward. A cheer, followed by laughter, filled the inside of the glowing sphere. They clutched one another as the bubble wiggled on the surface of the water.

"That was great!" Nick said when the joviality subsided. "Let's try it again." Nick called out the commands: "Left . . . Right . . . Left . . . Right." The ball rolled slowly on top of the water and through the darkness toward the far shore of the lake.

They quickly learned how important it was to work in perfect unison. If anyone got out of step, they all lost their balance and tumbled on top of one another, landing in a jumbled pile of arms and legs in the bottom of the bubble. It took much effort and grumbling to get everyone back on their feet and into place. "Cooperation and teamwork" became their rallying cry.

"Left . . . Right . . . Left . . . Right." As Nick called out the rhythmic commands, the glowing bubble rolled its way across the top of the smooth, black water and onto the shore at the far side of Loveless Lake. Once they were several feet past the shoreline, Nick withdrew his power that had kept them protected, and the four of them stood on dry land once again. A flood of relief filled each of them and they hugged one another.

Nancy turned back to look at the lake. "Well, I hope I never see you again," she said. As she did so, a loud moaning sound moved over the water.

chapter 14

Mantelia

The four humans looked at each other and let out a collective quiver. "What was that?" asked Nancy.

Nick shook his head. "The ghosts of the unicorns or the lake itself. Anything is possible here. It could even have been Hasbadana."

"I don't like this place. Let's get out of here," said Lynn with a shiver that traveled through her whole body.

"We still have a long way to travel," cautioned Bethany. "Let's take a few minutes to rest. And remember to get a drink of water. We have to cross the Desert of Despair."

"I'm not sure which sounds worse, drinking from that awful lake or crossing the Desert of Despair," moaned Lynn.

"The water really does taste bad, but it's wet," answered Bethany as she took Lynn's hand and pulled her to the edge of the lake. "Drink up. There is no other source of water until we reach home."

"'Home.' I love that word," said Nancy wistfully as she bent down and scooped the cold, black water into her mouth. The first taste was as awful as they had feared, and Lynn and Nancy both spit it out. Steeling themselves, they tried again and gulped down the water with much effort. Finally filled, they laid down on the pebbly shore to rest. Sleep soon overcame them.

Nick slept but not deeply and not restfully. When he did sleep, he dreamt of Urijah. He saw him in chains, bound and suffering. Nick awakened with a start, perspiration covering his body. Beside him, the girls seemed to be sleeping peacefully. He envied them.

When he tired of the tortured sleep, he awakened Bethany, Lynn, and, finally, Nancy. "Let's get going. I feel an urgency to free Urijah. Every minute he spends in captivity sickens me."

"I agree," answered Bethany as she stood and brushed the sand and pebbles from her tunic and out of her thick hair.

Lynn and Nancy stretched and struggled to their feet. They did not have the strength or stamina that members of the Legion of the Unicorn had been endowed with, and the journey was already taking its toll on them. Nick realized that crossing the Desert of Despair was going to be very difficult for them. Always their protector, he decided he would use his power to strengthen them. He placed his hands upon each of their heads— the right on Lynn's, the left on Nancy's—and sent his healing power into them. Their bodies were immediately infused with strength beyond their own. They both looked up at Nick and smiled warmly, grateful, once again, for their big brother.

With renewed energy and a great amount of determination, they started hiking. Bethany served as guide. They were surrounded by darkness and silence. The surface of the Desert of Despair was dry and cracked. Nothing moved. Nothing made a sound except for the soft crunching of their feet on the crusty sand.

It was difficult to know where they were going, as there were very few landmarks. Bethany pointed out an occasional rock formation or ravine but, as a whole, the desert was flat and dry. Nick walked along, searching for something to look at or listen to, hoping for anything that would alleviate the boredom of the environment and the worry that filled his heart. Their scope of vision was limited by the darkness beyond the reach of the light from their bodies. He strained his eyes and searched anyway. He found nothing except the things that Bethany pointed out, and those were few and far between.

"Let's sing a song," said Nancy, and she started singing some familiar songs from their childhood. Nick and Lynn joined in enthusiastically, marching along to the rhythm of the music. It helped to pass the time for a while, until Nancy noticed that Bethany was not singing with them. She stopped in midstanza, "Why aren't you singing with us, Bethany?"

"I don't know any of those songs."

"What? Everyone knows those songs. You can't have been a child without learning those songs."

"My mother never sang to me when I was a child."

Nancy stopped with her mouth open, looking aghast at Bethany. This was something she could not comprehend, having lived her short life in a home filled with love.

Nick realized that his sisters did not know Bethany's background. "Bethany, why don't you share your story with my sisters? I'm sure they would learn a lot from hearing it."

Bethany smiled, and an aura of peace surrounded her. She continued walking, but as she walked she quietly told her story, sometimes speaking only in a whisper. She told of her time on earth from her loveless childhood and life of hopelessness to the joyous reunion with her mother she experienced when Urijah sent her on her mission to find forgiveness. There was no bitterness in the telling, only compassion and love.

Lynn and Nancy listened intently. When Bethany finished her story, Lynn reached over and hugged her, holding her tightly for a long time. When she released her hold, she had tears streaming down her cheeks. Wiping the tears with the back of her hand, she said with a smile and a chuckle, "Well, now I understand how you came up with Loveless Lake and Desert of Despair for names."

Bethany laughed softly. "That was a different Bethany," she said with a smile.

They were now deep into the desert and all alone. "How much farther?" asked Nancy.

"Still quite a—" but Bethany didn't have time to finish her answer before a strange phenomenon caught their attention. The dark lines that marked the cracks in the crusty surface of the desert began to glow and emit light. At first they appeared to be a pale yellow, but slowly the light intensified until it became a bright, radiant red-orange. The four startled travelers stopped in their tracks and looked around. The cracks were gleaming all around them. There was no place to go to get away from them.

"What's happening?" shouted Nancy, panic evident in her voice.

"I don't know," answered Bethany. "I have never seen the desert do this before."

"Hasbadana?" guessed Lynn.

"Perhaps, but I have never seen him use light except as fire," answered Nick.

As if on cue, the cracks that had been glowing brightly began sending rays of light up into the sky. This was followed by fingers of flames lapping up through the cracks. Then the cracks themselves began separating and getting wider.

"Run!" yelled Nick as he grabbed Nancy's hand.

At once, all four of them began running, hoping to find the end of the burning desert and safety. It was futile. Ahead of them, behind them, and all around them, flames began leaping up through the crevasses even as the cracks continued to widen. Nick led Bethany and his sisters, with his hand still tightly clutching Nancy's, in a zigzag pattern as he leapt from one piece of gray, dry ground to the next, skimming over the tops of the flames. Ahead of him, Nick saw a fairly large piece of ground unmarred by fiery cracks. He headed in that direction and with a long leap, pulled Nancy over the final fissure. Right behind them, Lynn and Bethany came to a stop, hesitating at the edge of the crevasse.

"Come on," shouted Nick. "Jump!" Lynn looked up at Nick and then back down at the glowing fissure with its flames licking toward her like tongues. She rocked back on her right foot, took a step forward, and leaped, stretching her long legs across the widening gap. She landed gracefully beside Nick and Nancy, but Nick was only watching Bethany.

"Bethany, come now," he shouted across the flaming and enlarging divide.

Bethany looked from side to side, checking for any other way across. Seeing no other crossing point, she turned back to Nick. "I don't think I can make it."

"You can make it. You are a member of the legion. You have the power of love."

Closing her eyes and drawing upon the power deep inside of her, she drew in a long breath. She pushed herself up and into the air. As though she had wings, she floated slowly and softly across the flames even as they tickled her feet. Nick, Nancy, and Lynn watched with mouths agape.

When she touched down gently in front of Nick, he threw his arms around her. "I didn't know you could do that," he said, admiration in his voice.

She tilted her head back and looked into his eyes. Her entire face radiated as she said, "Neither did I."

Nick leaned down and gently kissed her lips. The celebration lasted but a brief moment. Like an elevator in descent, the island in the center of the flames upon which they were huddled began dropping slowly into the depths of the earth. Lynn and Nancy screamed as they watched the flames rise up all around them. They all looked up to see the black sky draw farther and farther away from them. Their podium dropped lower and lower, passing the flames and the molten lava as it descended far below the surface of the Dark Kingdom.

Once they had dropped below the hot, rumbling, hissing magma, they were lowered into a layer of black obsidian. The sides of the walls around them were shiny, and they could see their reflections on the walls as they dropped down deeper and deeper into the ground. Eventually, the black obsidian disappeared and was replaced by a white crystalline substance. Looking very much like giant salt crystals, the walls of the shaft down which they were moving were covered with geometric-shaped mineral deposits.

With a jolt, their platform came to a stop. The four immortal humans, still clinging to one another, looked around them. The crystal walls surrounded them on all sides except one. On this side, a tunnel opened up, but where it went it was impossible to tell. They looked at one another, uncertain just what to do. All three young women turned and rested their eyes upon Nick.

Not enthusiastic about taking the lead but realizing it was his responsibility, Nick stepped off the little island of crusty desert sand. "Let's go meet whoever has invited us down here."

One by one, each of the girls stepped silently down behind him, and all four started walking. The tunnel was quite round but not high enough to accommodate them in a standing position. They each had to walk through it by bending over at the waist. With hands supporting their aching backs and the light from Nick and Bethany's bodies lighting the way, they walked through the tunnel. The crystals around them glimmered and sparkled, reminding Nick of Urijah's horn.

After many minutes of walking, the tunnel opened up into a large room. Standing in the center of the room was a strange creature. It was about the size of a large dog but stood on its hind legs, its small front feet folded across its chest. Its face was ratlike, with a long, pointed nose. Its ears were on the side of its head. They were large and pointed and the top third flopped limply forward. Its perfectly round eyes were huge and bulging. They were a milky blue color, as though a film covered them. On either side of its pointed nose, several whiskers sprouted and extended nearly a foot out from its face. They were transparent, but the tips glowed with color like strands of fiber optics. Its hair-covered body was slim at the top but rotund from the waist down and bulged over its clawed feet. Extending beyond strong back legs was a long tail with a swath of coarse hair at the end, not unlike a donkey's.

"Welcome to the kingdom of Mantelia," he said in a voice far deeper than would be expected just by looking at the creature's narrow chest.

The talisman that hung around Nick's neck remained cool, indicating that Nick had nothing to fear from this strange-looking creature. He took a step ahead of the girls. "Mantelia? I have never heard of such a place."

"But of course not. We prefer to stay 'below the radar,' to use human speak, so that we might move about more freely. To use another of my favorite human phrases: 'Out of sight, out of mind.'" The odd-looking creature laughed heartily. "You see, we are the kingdom that belongs to the animals of the underground: from the tiny voles to the large wombats and every burrowing animal in between."

"But you don't look like any animal I have ever seen," answered Nick.

"That does not surprise me in the least. You see, I am a member of the most superior race of burrowers. We are the rulers of Mantelia. We are the Rodorix."

"And do you have a name?" asked Nick.

"Of course I do. You may call me Nehor."

"How do you do, Nehor? My name is Nicholas. I am a unicorn rider and a member of the Legion of the Unicorn."

"I know who you are. And you are accompanied by another unicorn rider and your two earthly sisters," said Nehor, nodding toward the young women who remained standing behind Nick.

"You seem to know a lot about us," said Nick guardedly.

"We make it our business to know what is happening in all of the kingdoms. Knowledge is the source of power, do you not agree?"

"If it is used to create wisdom."

"Ha," he laughed deeply in his throat. "Spoken like a true unicorn."

Bethany stepped up beside Nick. "I trust it was you that we must thank for rescuing us from the flames."

"Thank me if you wish. But it was the Rodorix that sent the flames in the first place so, perhaps, your gratitude is misplaced."

"Why would you do such a thing?" asked Lynn, joining the conversation now.

Nehor shrugged his narrow shoulders and raised his short front legs in a show of nonchalance. "We were merely following orders."

"Whose orders?" demanded Nick, a bit too aggressively.

"Why, the orders given by Nebbish, the lord of Mantelia."

"I gather your Lord Nebbish sent forth the flames in order to bring us down here," said Bethany.

"I gather," answered Nehor curtly.

"Why would he want us brought here anyway?" she continued.

"Perhaps you should ask him yourself. He is awaiting your timely arrival. Let us delay no longer. We would not want to upset him. He can be very distasteful when he is angered." Nehor turned on his haunches and lowered his short front legs. In a motion reminiscent of a kangaroo on all fours, Nehor led them through another tunnel, his long flowing tail dragging behind him.

Chapter 15

Nebbish

They followed Nehor through numerous twisting and turning tunnels and entered and exited several rooms, most of which were inhabited by one type of underground animal or another. Nick noticed that all of the animals were being monitored by a threatening-looking Rodorix. He thought this was strange and wondered why the Rodorix needed to keep guard over the other animals.

As the humans entered a chamber, they were able to give their backs a rest by standing upright. Even the largest of the rooms were still not all that high. They could easily touch the ceiling if they reached up with their hands.

The ceilings of each room were a web of roots, some as thin as a hair, others as thick as a boa constrictor. The roots dripped a golden liquid. Nick noticed that the liquid was being collected in shallow bowls and from these bowls several of the animals were seen drinking.

However, upon the arrival of the humans in a warren, the animals gathered there stopped what they were doing and scurried to their respective holes. Each appeared to have their own private opening that had been dug into the crystal walls. Some of the burrows were tiny and others very large, each designed to fit the animal that called it home. Once inside the safety of their shelter, they turned and watched the strange visitors pass through the room.

"I must apologize for the shyness of our inhabitants. It is hard to overcome earthly habits. In Mantelia, they have no exposure to humans. The older animals will greet you in a friendlier manner," said Nehor. "They have learned to overcome the natural animal."

Nehor escorted them into a large crystal room quite different from any rooms they had seen thus far. It had a bright glowing orb in one corner, reminiscent of the sun. A cloudlike mist floated across the ceiling. From some of the clouds, flashes of lightning were seen and heard while drops of water fell from other clouds. In one corner, a pile of white dust was accumulating below the clouds from which white powder continuously fell. No one inhabited this room.

"What room is this?" asked Nancy.

Looking around and shaking his head, Nehor responded, "This chamber belongs to the groundhogs. They have some silly idea that they can predict the weather. They are continually practicing. Since it is cloudy right now, they should be coming out of their burrows soon."

Nehor guided them through another crystal warren. The Rodorix that stood guard at the entrance turned to face them. "What have we here, Nehor?" the guard asked, suspicion dripping from his voice.

"I am helping these humans flee from the Dark Kingdom," was Nehor's curt reply, insulted that he would be questioned.

A blind mole curled in a ball just in front of them lifted his head with a jerk. "Flea? Did someone say 'flea?'"

Suddenly, all around the room, moles woke up.

"Flea?"

"Flea!"

"Who has fleas?"

"I don't have any fleas! Do you have fleas?"

Nehor rolled his eyes and shook his head. "Moles. They are so stupid," he said as he walked across the burrow. He directed them out of the warren, leaving a roomful of moles sitting on their round bottoms, scratching themselves.

"Why are the Rodorix guarding them?" asked Nick.

Nehor stopped and looked around at Nick with a look of suspicion. "Why do you say that?"

"Well, I noticed the Rodorix in each room didn't seem exactly benevolent toward the animals."

"Why should they be? They must keep all of these rodents under control," responded Nehor brusquely. His manner softened slightly. "You must realize that we have to keep order in the kingdom." Feeling the need to change the subject, Nehor asked, "Now, can I interest you in some Mantelia nectar? It is quite refreshing and very nutritious." He bent down and picked up a bowl with his long, claw-like fingers and offered it to them. The bowl contained a shimmering golden liquid.

Bethany reached out her hands first. Pressing the bowl to her lips, she tipped it up and took a tiny sip. She looked over at Nick as she savored the taste in her mouth then immediately took another drink. "Oh my! This is delicious," she said as she took yet another big swallow before passing the bowl over to Lynn.

Lynn, encouraged by Bethany's response, took a long draft. She closed her eyes and smiled widely as she relished the flavor in her mouth. "Try this, Nancy. You are going to love it," she said as she passed it over to her little sister.

Nancy took a big swallow, then another and another.

"Hey, slow down. Leave some for me," said Nick with a laugh.

"You needn't worry. We have a never-ending supply," said Nehor, delighted by their response.

Nancy handed the bowl over to Nick and watched him with a smile as he took a sip. Nick was surprised by the sweet, fruity taste of the golden liquid. He turned to Nehor. "That is the most delicious drink I have ever tasted. What is it?"

"It is made from the root sap of all of the living plants. The different flavors blend together and make our special potion. It is similar to the way bees make honey from flower nectar." He motioned up toward the maze of roots intertwined above them. All heads turned upward and, as they did so, drips of root nectar fell on their faces. They all laughed as they wiped the liquid out of their eyes and off their cheeks. With delight, they licked the delicious juice from their hands.

"Tell me, Nehor. Are we still beneath the Dark Kingdom?" asked Bethany as she licked the Mantelia nectar off her last fingers.

Nehor stopped and looked around as he calculated their location. "At this point, we should be beneath the forest that borders the Animal Kingdom. So, yes, we are still beneath the Dark Kingdom."

"Does your kingdom extend as far as Celestia?" asked Nick, wiping the Mantelia nectar from his face.

"Oh my, yes. We go back and forth anywhere we want. Dark Kingdom, Animal Kingdom, Celestia—it makes no difference to us." He raised his pointed chin and looked down at them with an air of superiority. "We refuse to take sides."

"Then, once we have met with your lord, will you be able to help us get home through your maze of tunnels?" asked Nick as they lowered their heads to enter yet another burrow.

"If that is Nebbish's desire."

A stab of panic went through Nick. What if Nebbish kept them here as his prisoners? They would have simply gone from one entombment to another. Would Urijah's sacrifice have been in vain? He looked over at Bethany, whose face expressed the same concern. With relief, he noticed that his talisman remained cool, signifying that, at least for the present, they were not in danger.

Their journey through the labyrinth finally came to an end at a double set of sparkling white doors, the first doors they had yet seen in Mantelia.

"This is Nebbish's chambers. You are to wait here while I let him know you have arrived."

Nehor tapped his clawed front feet on the door. In a moment it opened slightly and he entered, walking on his hind legs. The doors closed quickly, catching the last half of his long tail. With jerking motions, the hairs of the tail were pulled through the door.

Nick stood and stared at the white doors that were now closed to him. He narrowed his eyes and stepped closer to examine the intricate design carved in the stone from which the doors were made. He studied it carefully and realized it was a map. In the center of the map was a circle. Coming out in all directions flowed a maze of what looked like roads.

Bethany stepped up beside him. "What are you looking at?"

"Look at the carvings on this door. They seem to be depicting a map. Look at all the roads."

Bethany examined the carving. "Not roads," she finally said. "Tunnels."

Nick looked at her in admiration. "You're right! It is a map of the underworld."

"That's right," she said. "And we are standing in front of Nebbish's chambers right in the center," she said, tapping her finger on the circle.

Lynn and Nancy stepped up beside them and looked at the map. "Do you think this map could help us escape from here?" asked Nancy.

Nick studied the map again. Slowly he shook his head. "I can't tell which way we came from or which way we should go from here," he said with frustration. "We could end up right back in the Dark Kingdom if we went the wrong way."

The four humans were bent over with their noses nearly touching the door when it suddenly opened. Nick and Bethany felt their talismans get warm. They stood up abruptly. Nehor stood in front of them with a look of suspicion on his face.

"We noticed the beautiful carvings on the door. We assume that is a diagram of the Underground Kingdom," said Nick.

Nehor's milky blue eyes studied them. "Yes, I'm sure you *did* notice the map. However, don't think you can find your way out of the Underground Kingdom on your own. You would be lost for centuries in the labyrinth," answered Nehor with an air of arrogance. "Now, follow me. Nebbish is ready to speak to you." Nehor turned on his hind legs, his long tail swishing around, brushing the floor.

Nick and the young women followed him into the room behind the doors, the talisman around his neck getting warmer with each step. They entered an enormous round chamber, which was not at all what Nick expected. He assumed it would be hollowed out of the same white crystal that all the tunnels and burrows had been carved from. But not this room. This room was bright red and sparkled like a giant ruby. The ceiling was again a web of intertwined roots, but all of these roots were as red as the rest of the room. The roots extended down the walls in beautiful curving designs. It felt to Nick as though he and his companions were standing in the middle of a crimson forest. In the very center of the room was a semicircle of stalactites and stalagmites that just touched one another. They sparkled as if made from diamonds, and all of the tiny flat angles on the surface of the formations reflected the red from the walls. It was from this grand, central focal-point of the room, on a raised dais, that the lord of the Underground sat upon his throne and watched the four humans enter.

Nehor escorted them to the base of the platform and lowered himself down onto his short front paws. He curled his pointy face back to look at the visitors and motioned with his head for them to bow as well. They obediently bowed at the waist before quickly standing upright again. Nehor, still in the crouching position, cleared his throat and motioned for them to bow again. Nick looked at the girls, shrugged his shoulders, and bowed again, this time remaining in the position of obeisance, waiting for any indication that they could stand again.

They remained in this position while Nebbish addressed them. Getting right to the matter at hand, the lord of the Underground spoke in a low, rumbling voice. Nick raised his eyes briefly and noticed that Nebbish was a much larger Rodorix than Nehor. He was silver in color, and his fiber optic–like whiskers were glowing brightly in ever-changing colors. He was staring down at them with his milky-blue eyes. "I have brought you here for a very important purpose, not that I have to justify my actions, you understand. But I felt you might appreciate knowing why you are here so you might be able to fulfill the assignment you will be given in an efficient and expedient manner."

He paused for a moment, and Nick started to raise his head to look directly at their . . . Nick wasn't sure what to call him. Was he their host or their warden? As Nick lifted his head,

Nehor cleared his throat loudly from his crouching position, and the young unicorn rider immediately dropped his head back down.

Nebbish continued. "I am the lord of the Underground. Few have ever had the privilege of being in my presence." Lynn, standing bent over beside Nick, gave a snort of derision. Nehor turned his head and glared at her. Nebbish ignored it. "It seems that we of the Rodorix race are facing a difficult problem that we have not been able to solve ourselves." Nebbish raised his short front legs to his face, licked his paws, and groomed his long, lighted whiskers before he spoke again. "It seems that our young have developed a . . . what shall I call it? A malady. You see, they are born, start to grow, and then begin shrinking. We do not know what is causing this problem nor have we been able to figure out how to cure it. That is why we have brought you here. With your healing powers we are hopeful you can be of assistance to us."

Nick raised his head while staying in the crouched-over position. "We would be honored to use our powers to help you if we can."

"I hoped as much," said the lord of the Underground Kingdom. His voice and demeanor softened immediately. "Nehor, take our guests to the nursery and let them begin without delay."

"Yes, my lord," said Nehor as he scooted backward. When he bumped into Nick, he whispered, "Back up."

The four visitors remained in their bowed position even as they shuffled their feet backward. When they had nearly backed into the doors, Nehor stood, turned around, and walked out the door. Nick stood as well, assuming it must be acceptable protocol if Nehor was doing it. He turned and walked behind Nehor and out the white, stone doors that stood open for them.

They followed Nehor through another maze of tunnels and burrows until they arrived in a room filled with little piles of straw and leaves. Nestled in each pile were several, perhaps as many as a dozen, tiny Rodorix, identical in shape as their elders but with hairless bodies and hairless, rat-like tails. Several Rodorix, who seemed to be tending the infants, were scurrying around the room. Once the group of humans with Nehor as their guide entered, all movement stopped and all eyes turned to the strangers.

After a moment of awkward silence, one of the attendees stepped up to Nehor. "What is the meaning of this, Nehor? Who are these humans, and why have you brought them here?"

"We are here under the direction of Nebbish. This is Nicholas and Bethany, the unicorn riders you have surely heard about," he said as he motioned toward them. Nick nodded his head politely.

"And why would Lord Nebbish send them here?" asked the nurse curtly.

"He believes they have the power to heal our infants."

Realization dawned on the Rodorix, and a smile appeared beneath her pointed nose. She turned toward Nick and Bethany, a sparkle in her pale blue eyes. "Do you really think you can heal our babies?"

"We will do our best," replied Nick, compassion welling up in his heart.

"I surely hope so. Please, follow me," the Rodorix said, turning on the heels of her clawed back feet, her tail swirling around behind her. She walked across the burrow to the far side of the cavern where several nurses were huddled around a mound of straw. She turned and looked at Nick and Bethany, tears welling up in her eyes. "These are the worst of our patients." She turned halfway and motioned with her short front leg.

Nick and Bethany, with Lynn and Nancy right behind them, leaned over and peered into the mound. Huddled together in a tight ball were several tiny Rodorix, much smaller than the ones in the front nests. They reminded Nick of raisins both because of their size and because of the wrinkles that covered their bodies.

"These were the first to be born with whatever disease is causing them to shrink. If we wait much longer, I fear they will be so tiny we won't even be able to see them, let alone care for them," lamented one of the nurses.

Nick turned to Bethany. "Let's get to work," he said, feeling the same urgency the nurses felt. Nick and Bethany closed their eyes and focused on the love they carried with them. They placed their fingers over the babies and commanded them to be healed. Rays of light jumped from their fingertips and formed a warm halo around the tiny Rodorix. The babies all started squeaking and squirming in response to the power being sent into them. The two unicorn riders held their position for several minutes, filling each tiny body with the love needed to heal whatever infirmity was destroying them.

Nick and Bethany followed the nursemaids around the burrow, sending their power into each litter of tiny babies. By the time they were done, the once silent room was filled with the tiny squeaks of hundreds of miniature Rodorix babies.

After working over the last nest, Nick and Bethany collapsed in exhaustion. Lynn and Nancy were immediately at their sides, cradling them in their arms. Nehor stepped forward and looked down at them. "Have you done it? Are they healed?"

Nick looked up into the filmy blue eyes. "Yes, Nehor, they are healed."

"How can you be sure?"

"I felt it."

"I am not sure that will be enough evidence for Nebbish."

"Then he will just have to see what happens," replied Nick with confidence.

"I, for one, thank you for your efforts on their behalf," said the first nurse.

"You are welcome, my friend," said Bethany with a warm smile as she reached up and took a hold of the Rodorix's front paw. A bond of mutual admiration instantly formed between these two females from different species. They both smiled as they looked deeply into one another's eyes.

"Well," interjected Nehor, "as soon as you have rested, I would like to return to Nebbish's chambers and report on what you have done."

Nick gathered his strength and jumped up, the thought of finally returning to Celestia filling him with much-needed energy. He was eager for them to get on their way. "Yes, Nehor, let's get going," he said as he turned and helped Bethany to her feet.

Back through the maze, the little group traveled until they found themselves standing in front of the crystal doors once again. The same ritual was repeated, with Nehor entering first. However, he managed to get his tail through the opening without it getting caught this time. By the time Nick and his companions were invited into the red chamber, Nick had decided his back was not going to endure any more bending, and he walked in straight and tall and remained that way as he addressed Nebbish.

Nebbish eyed him suspiciously as the impetuous young man spoke. "We have done as you have asked, Lord Nebbish. We have used our powers to heal your infants. I must add that it was an honor to do so. However, it is imperative that we return to Celestia immediately. If you would be so kind as to provide us with a guide through your kingdom, we would be forever grateful."

Nebbish eyed Nick with a look of both curiosity and respect. When he spoke, his deep voice rumbled through the large, circular room and caused the stalactites and stalagmites to shake. "I will release you when I am convinced that our young are healed, and not a moment before." Nick could feel his talisman getting warm once again.

Nehor, who had pressed his face to the floor, began scooting backward in an effort to make a hasty exit. But Nick stood his ground. "Nebbish, it is imperative that we leave now. Urijah is being held prisoner by Hasbadana and we need to return to Celestia to find a way to help him."

"That is not my problem, young unicorn rider. My only concern is the welfare of the Rodorix race and the burrowing animals that make up my Underground Kingdom. I will release you when I am persuaded that you have done your assigned task. Nehor, take our guests to their chambers."

Nick stood still for a moment and glared at Nebbish. The lord of the Underground Kingdom turned his back. Bethany came up beside Nick, slipped her arm through his, and gently pulled him back toward the door. In disgust, Nick turned and stomped out of the red room.

Nehor led them down yet another tunnel. This tunnel made a dead end in a small burrow. "You may stay here until Nebbish calls for you again. Make yourselves comfortable," said Nehor before he left them alone.

The four weary travelers stood in the middle of the empty burrow. "Well, this is lovely," said Lynn. "Home, sweet home."

"Okay, so here we are. We might as well make the best of it," chirped Nancy. "Nick, I'm starving. Can you make us some food?"

While Nick called forth food—breads, cheese, fruits, and vegetables—Bethany made each of them a soft bed of straw and leaves, a larger version of the nests in the nursery. After eating until they were satisfied, they each selected a bed and laid their exhausted bodies down. Nick stretched out on his back with his arms folded under his head. He said nothing as he stared up at the roots that covered the ceiling and tried to calm his anxious heart and mind. It was too painful to think about Urijah, so he allowed his thoughts to dwell on Lazari. How he wished his unicorn were here with him. Lazari always knew how to calm him. At last, Nick closed his eyes and a deep sleep came over him.

Morning was a relative term in Mantelia. It was simply the time of day when one woke up. The four humans ate breakfast then allowed Bethany to command their clothing, skin, and hair to clean itself. When Bethany was done, they all felt refreshed, clean, and rested. At that moment, they heard the shuffling and clicking sound that Rodorix feet made as they scurried along the tunnels. The sound was clearly coming toward them through the crystal tunnel.

Nehor burst into their burrow accompanied by several of the nursemaids. "They are well!" he exclaimed. "Our infants are well," he repeated with excitement.

The nursemaids fell all over Nick and Bethany, "Oh, dear unicorn riders, we can't thank you enough. You have healed our babies."

Nick looked over the Rodorix surrounding him to Nehor. "Does this mean we are free to go?"

"It does. Nebbish has released you and given me permission to take you wherever you would like to go."

Lynn and Nancy bounced up and down and squealed with delight. Nick looked over at Bethany who was still being fawned over by the Rodorix nursemaids. She looked up, her face beaming. He loved seeing the joy in her face. "Let's go," he mouthed. She nodded.

After saying their goodbyes, Nick asked Nehor to take them to the rose garden where they had entered the Dark Kingdom. He knew that Shema and Lazari would be faithfully waiting for them there. Nehor set off immediately, and the four excited travelers followed, nearly stepping on his long tail hairs.

They crouched through several tunnels, the ache in their backs returning, when Nehor finally stopped in a burrow. "The rose garden is right above us. You will notice the many bowls collecting nectar from here. We love the flavor the roots of the roses make." Nick, Bethany, Lynn, and Nancy all looked up. The ceiling above them appeared like all the rest. How their Rodorix guide could tell one from the other was beyond their comprehension.

As they watched in stunned silence, Nehor stood on his back legs and leapt to the ceiling, gripping the intertwined roots like a playground jungle gym. He placed the tip of his nose against the ceiling, and his whiskers began twirling in a blaze of colored lights. Like a chainsaw, his whiskers cut the roots into a symmetrical circle. Next, he poked his nose through the roots and started working on the crystal. As he did so, the ceiling began melting. Globs of white crystal started dripping down from above like big drops of melted sugar. As they did so, the hole in the ceiling grew bigger. Nehor kept drilling as he worked his way up. He crawled up the vertical tunnel he was drilling until he was out of sight, leaving a smooth-sided shaft behind him. After several minutes of drilling Rodorix style, a ray of sunlight poured down the tube. Nick looked up with so much excitement, he could hardly contain himself.

With a bump, Nehor dropped out of the shaft and landed on the floor in front of them. "It's all yours," he said with a sweeping motion of his short front arms.

Nick, remembering Bethany's ability to float across the flaming crevasse, focused his power on Nancy. With a squeal of delight, her body began floating up and into the tube. Next he sent Lynn.

Just as he turned his attention on Bethany, he saw her hold up her hand. "I'll do it myself," she said with a smile. Silently, she floated up and out of sight.

As Nick was about to lift off, Nehor called his name. Nick stopped and looked down at the Rodorix. "Nicholas, the unicorn rider, thank you for helping us. If we can ever be of assistance to you, please let us know."

Nick smiled and nodded. "Thank you, Nehor. But how would I reach you?"

"We know whenever the surface of the ground is broken. If you dig a hole in the soil with a golden spade and insert this lavender crystal into the opening, we will know you are in need of our assistance."

Nehor stepped forward and handed Nick a small lavender crystal. Nick turned it over and over in his fingers as he examined its beautifully carved sides. He slipped it into his shoulder pouch that also contained the invisible clover. He reached out and took hold of Nehor's slender front paw. "Thank you, Nehor. There may very well come a time when you can help me." He lifted his hand in a military salute and sent his body up through the crystal duct. Waiting anxiously in the rose garden above him was his beloved unicorn.

Chapter 16

Home Again

While Nick and Bethany struggled to get home through the Dark Kingdom and Mantelia, Lazari and Shema paced back and forth in the rose garden nervously awaiting their return. Every animal in the Animal Kingdom and every unicorn in Celestia was keenly aware of Urijah's sacrifice on behalf of the humans. Each animal carried a heavy heart and mourned the loss of their leader and exemplar. Additionally, Lazari and Shema worried about the unexpected delay in the return of their riders. Had they not been unicorns, their pacing back and forth would have worn an unsightly path in front of the lattice archway. Instead, the unicorns' steps didn't make a mark on the blades of grass. Lazari had been particularly agitated that he was not able to communicate with Nick through his thoughts. Hasbadana, with his increased power, had found a way to block their thoughts from one another.

As Lazari and Shema completed another lap around the garden, a high-pitched buzzing sound reached their ears. They stopped and stared. Right in front of them, the garden dirt started to wiggle and then erupted upward like a geyser. When the dust settled, a strange-looking animal with a pointed nose that supported glowing, whirling whiskers popped its head out of the hole that now disfigured the appearance of the pristine garden. In the time it took Lazari and Shema to throw up their heads and blink their eyes, the ugly creature was gone. Lazari and Shema looked at each other in curiosity and concern. Just as they started to step forward to investigate the newly formed hole in the ground, Nancy rose up out of the opening.

Nick was the last of the four humans to rise out of the gopher-like hole that had marred the beautiful rose gardens. Lazari was standing with his front hooves placed firmly on either side of the hole, his head hanging down. Nick gripped his sparkling amber horn, and his unicorn lifted him up and tossed him onto his back. Nick leaned forward and draped an arm on either side of the unicorn's sleek, dark neck. "Lazari! I am so happy to see you again."

Lazari turned his neck and nuzzled Nick's foot. *And I, you.*

There were times I wasn't sure I would ever see you again, whispered Nick in his thoughts.

I would never have let that happen. You are my rider. I am incomplete without you, responded Lazari, love gleaming from his eyes.

In a matter of minutes, Mastis galloped into the garden, breathing hard for the first time since Nick had known him. "You have returned. I heard your thoughts in the garden. I must say, I am so relieved." Yet the homecoming celebration was short-lived as he continued speaking. "You must come with me to meet with the council at once."

Bethany vaulted onto Shema's golden back and grasped her flowing white mane. Mastis bent his left front leg and lowered his sparkling body so Lynn and Nancy could easily climb on his back. Once they were settled—Nancy gripping the black mane and Lynn holding onto Nancy—the magnificent unicorn leaped forward in a gallop, running so fast that all the flowers and trees around them disappeared in a blur of color.

As they galloped across the Animal Kingdom, Mastis explained to Nicholas and Bethany that, due to the absence of Urijah, the Council of the Twelve Ancients had assumed the leadership role in Celestia. They continued with their responsibilities as a governing body and in leading the Legion of the Unicorn as it fulfilled its assignments to serve the animals.

As they entered Celestia, Nick drew in a quick breath. The beautiful land of the unicorns seemed muted. The music that filled the air was still there, but it seemed to float slowly and tentatively to their ears. To their eyes, the colors were subdued. Even the bejeweled doors that provided access to the council chambers didn't sparkle as they had before. Nick looked around him with a tremendous amount of melancholy, saddened by the changes that were so obvious all around him.

Everything is missing Urijah, said Mastis to Nick, through his thoughts.

They entered the antechamber of the council room. The stars that fell from the dome above them sparkled once but disappeared before they reached the mosaic floor. The unicorns that hustled past them, moving from one task to another, acknowledged the unicorns and their riders with a brief nod of their heads, but their eyes lacked their customary twinkle.

As soon as they reached the beautiful gold doors of the council chambers, the two chestnut guards who had watched them approach bowed in the customary unicorn fashion by bending their right legs until their knees touched the ground, dropping their heads and touching their horns to the floor. Immediately they stood, turned toward the doors, which opened widely, and directed the group into the room that provided the meeting place for the Council of the Twelve Ancients.

Arranged on the raised dais were twelve sparkling unicorns, six on either side of an ominous empty space. The unicorn that stood to the right of the place once occupied by Urijah stepped forward. "Welcome, my friends," said Helam. "We are so thankful for your safe return from the Dark Kingdom. I can't express how pleased we were to hear that you had finally arrived home."

The two unicorn riders slid off their partners' backs and bowed to Helam and the council. Mastis, Lazari, and Shema did the same. Nick stood up and took a deep breath in an effort to control his emotions. "Thank you, Helam. How I wish it were under different circumstances."

"As do we, my son, as do we." Helam dropped his head for a moment. When he lifted it again, Nick could see a tear slowly glide down his elegant face. But, in a businesslike manner, Helam continued speaking. "As the senior member of the council, I will conduct this interview. Please recount for us, if you will, all that transpired in the Dark Kingdom."

Nick looked over at Bethany. She responded by smiling warmly at him, reaching over and taking his hand in hers. She nodded her head by way of encouragement. Nick turned his attention back to the Council of the Twelve Ancients and began his story.

The young unicorn rider recounted all that happened from the moment they were greeted at the doors of Valhalla by Hasbadana and his guards. The council listened with rapt attention. Nick described the swirling cones of mist that kept Lynn and Nancy suspended in the air and that also encapsulated him and Bethany.

"Time cannot be measured in the Dark Kingdom, and even if it could be, I was in no state to be able to keep track of it. I am sorry, but it is impossible for me to give an account of how long we were captive in the cone of mist. But when I awoke from the stupor I was in, Urijah was in the room with us . . . bound in chains."

"In chains?" said one of the council members, clearly shocked.

"Yes. Hasbadana has Urijah encircled in thick, heavy chains."

"But why?" asked another. "Surely Hasbadana knows that Urijah will not attempt to escape once he has given his word."

Bethany stepped forward. "May I give you my opinion?"

"Please," responded Helam with a nod of his sparkling head.

"I believe Hasbadana takes great joy in seeing Urijah in such a humiliating condition. Holding Urijah bound in chains places Hasbadana in a position of power and prestige in front of his army."

"Ah . . ." said Helam slowly. "Politics. Indeed, appearances are very important to such a leader as he, far more important than principle."

"Yes. Exactly," agreed Bethany.

"Other than the cruel and unnecessary restraints, do you believe Hasbadana will treat Urijah maliciously?" asked Helam.

"While I am not surprised by the chains, I would be surprised if he was cruel to Urijah in any other way. Deep within Hasbadana, while it may not be love, there is certainly an admiration for Urijah. Respect, perhaps. This, of course, mingles with jealousy and resentment," said Bethany, with knotted brow.

Nick watched her as she carefully picked her words, thinking how beautiful she looked, deep in thought. He squeezed her hand in support and affection. With great effort, he turned away from Bethany and focused once again on the conversation taking place in the council chambers.

Helam turned back to Nick. "Nicholas, please continue with your account."

Nick told of the adventures returning home. The unicorn leaders were especially interested to learn that their powers to control the elements were now being blocked by Hasbadana. Their heads lifted and ears pricked forward when Nick began recounting their experience in Mantelia.

"You entered Mantelia?" said one.

"Well, not by choice. We kind of fell into it, you might say."

"No other unicorn, except Urijah, has ever been invited into Mantelia," said Helam by way of explanation for their startled reaction. "So did you meet Nebbish, the leader of the Rodorix?"

"Yes, my lord. He had brought us to his kingdom to use our healing powers on their infants."

All of the council members nodded with understanding and admiration for this young unicorn rider.

"And were you able to heal them?" asked Helam.

"Yes. Had we not been successful, we would still be there as his prisoners."

"Ah, that sounds like the Nebbish we have heard about. Tell us about his kingdom. How far-reaching is it?"

"It extends beneath the Dark Kingdom, the Animal Kingdom, and . . ."

"Celestia?" interjected a council member.

"Yes. Even beneath Celestia."

The unicorns looked back and forth at one another, their eyes open wide with amazement.

Helam spoke up once again. "I trust you have made a valuable friend in Nebbish."

"Yes, my lord. The Rodorix have promised to help me if needed, and they have given me instructions on how to reach them."

Helam and the council nodded their approval. "Tell me, Nicholas, have you been inspired with a plan regarding our beloved Urijah?"

"Yes, Helam." Nick paused, suddenly fearing that his plan may seem sophomoric to such wise leaders as these. Taking a deep breath, he continued. "I believe we need to heal Hasbadana."

All the council members reared their heads back and looked at Nick with incredulity. "And just how will we do that?" asked one while looking down his long nose at the young rider.

"I don't know. I was hoping you could give me some guidance."

Silence filled the room as the council conversed silently through their thoughts. Heads nodded, sending forelocks bouncing from one side of a glistening horn to the other. Front hooves silently pawed the ground, and long, flowing tails swished back and forth in signs of apprehension. Helam studied his beloved associates as he listened to, and carefully considered, their thoughts. Nick and Bethany waited silently. Nick felt his hands sweating and rubbed them on his pants. He found some comfort in the fact that at least the council was giving his suggestion serious consideration.

Finally, all sparkling heads turned toward the two young riders and their unicorns. Helam spoke. "We believe that you may, indeed, have been inspired with a viable solution. However, we do not have the answer as to how that might be done. We would like you to meet with Animara."

"Animara?" asked Nick.

"Yes. Animara is the patriarch of the fairies. He alone holds the keys to all of the healing powers. His authority to heal is far greater than any bestowed upon the unicorns."

Excitement and hope filled Nick's breast. He looked back and forth between Lazari and Bethany, his eyes twinkling.

— chapter 17 —

Animara

Gidoni, the lovely, pale green fairy, led Nick, on Lazari, and Bethany, on Shema, deep into the lush forest of Celestia. Nick breathed in the spicy aroma of the pines and fir trees. He smiled as he watched them move apart to let them pass. He loved feeling the strength of his unicorn beneath him. He let his body move with the rhythmic rocking of Lazari's canter as they moved across the forest floor. The warm breeze kissed his face and tousled his hair.

Just ahead, Gidoni flew in front of the riders and their unicorns at their eye level. After quite a long journey, the little group entered an area Nick had never seen before. The evergreen pines, firs, and cedars gave way to deciduous flowering trees. These trees shed their leaves during the night and burst forth with fresh leaves and blossoms by the time the sun broke the horizon each morning. Their discarded leaves and petals left the ground beneath them feeling like a thickly padded and deliciously perfumed carpet.

Music from hundreds of whirling fairy wings filled the air. Nick looked up to see dozens of fairies flitting from tree to tree, flower to flower, keeping pace with the riders and their unicorns as they sped along. At times, Gidoni greeted one fairy or another. All seemed to know and revere him.

Very gradually, almost imperceptibly, the ground upon which they were traveling began to rise. The multicolored trees gave way to the most beautiful green and white forest one could ever imagine. Nick had never seen anything like it. The lower level of the woods and up to about the height of the unicorns' bellies was covered with the broad leaves of a flowering hemlock. Above the leaves, large, white flowers stood on tall, stiff stems. The flower heads were each nearly a foot across. Their faces were made up of hundreds of tiny blossoms that formed an intricate, lacy pattern that would send envy into the hearts of the famous French lace makers in Normandy. Perhaps most dramatic and beautiful of all were the tall, thick trunks of the aspen trees that rose above the flowering hemlocks. Their white trunks sparkled, pulsating with a light that glowed and dimmed in a rhythm that matched the music in the air. Nick's eye traveled up the trunks to the green canopy of aspen leaves. The leaves twisted and turned in the gentle breeze above their heads.

"It is so beautiful," he whispered reverently.

Yes, it is, responded Lazari silently.

Nick looked over at Bethany. She, too, was overwhelmed with the beauty of the green and white forest. Tears streamed down her cheeks as she stared up at the gentle foliage-covered hillside.

Once they reached the top of the hill, the aspens and flowering hemlock parted and formed a circular clearing in the center of which was an ancient, thick, and twisted tree. Gidoni led them through the clearing and stopped in front of the tree. The base of the trunk was huge with curling roots extending out in all directions. Its bark was nearly purple in color, reminding Nick of the color of an eggplant. Its leaves were a bright, fluorescent green. The flowers that separated the leaves and covered the gnarly branches were white with bright pink centers. The blossoms opened and shut their petals like a butterfly's wings, making the tree appear to be in constant motion. Nick stared up at the magical tree, his mouth agape. He had never seen a tree so fascinating and beautiful. An aura of light and power seemed to emanate from every inch of the tree. Nick was drawn to it as though being pulled by invisible bands. He had never felt such an overwhelming influence.

Nick was not the only thing attracted to the tree. All the trees, bushes, and flowers around it leaned in toward this grandest of all members of the plant kingdom.

"This is Animara's home," said Gidoni in quiet reverence. "Animara is the holder of all the healing keys that he disperses among the fairies. You must wait here and I will go up to inquire about obtaining an audience with him."

Without speaking aloud, Nick and Lazari exchanged thoughts. *Have you ever seen anything so beautiful?*

No, never. I feel like I want to stay here forever.

As do I.

Which of the two spoke first it was impossible to say, and not necessary, as their thoughts were identical and were a mirror image of one another.

Gidoni returned quickly with a smile on his face. In his high-pitched voice he announced excitedly, "Animara will see both Nicholas and Bethany immediately."

Nick looked over at Bethany and then leaned his head back, gazing up to the top of the tree to where he had seen Gidoni fly. A perplexed expression covered his face as he turned back to Gidoni.

Gidoni, sensing his concern, laughed. "Do not worry. I will get you up there."

Gidoni flew over their heads in a figure eight pattern while chanting some strange words from the fairy language. Following this, he headed for the highest branches of the tree. Nick and Bethany were instantly lifted off their unicorns and carried perhaps thirty feet above the ground behind the little green fairy. Their bodies were gently lowered down onto a thick branch that extended out from the trunk of the tree in a perpendicular position. Nick placed a protective arm around Bethany and, hesitant to look down, turned instead to look at the trunk of the tree. There, between the thick folds of the purple bark, was a lovely little door. It was no more than a foot in height and rather narrow. The lovely entry was golden in color and had tiny carvings of fairies all over its surface. Nick turned to look at Gidoni. "Will he be coming out?"

Gidoni chuckled with his musical laugh again. "Oh, no. You must go in." Instantly, a dozen fairies appeared over their heads singing a beautiful song in the ancient language of the fairies. With a sizzling and popping sound, Nick and Bethany were instantly reduced to the size of the fairies. For a moment, all went black. When Nick was able to finally gather his senses about him, he looked down at his body in amazement. He could not have been more than eight inches tall. He patted his body to see if all of it was still there. He looked over at Bethany, who was slightly smaller. The leaves and flowers on the branches around him seemed enormous, their pistils and stamens as large as trumpets. Dewdrops seemed as large as the basketballs he had played with during his earth life.

He turned his head and looked at the trunk of the tree. There, in front of them, was the tiny golden door, now taller than they were. The beautiful carvings of fairies that decorated the door were now easy to decipher. They depicted the life of a fairy from childhood in the protective shelter of the daylilies, to their training and, finally, adulthood serving as the messengers of Celestia. As he looked at the door, it opened, and there stood a very old fairy. He was once the same height as the other fairies, but now his shoulders were hunched over, making him appear shorter. The little old fairy motioned them inside with his wrinkled hand, which extended from its position at the end of his thin arm.

Nick reached behind him, grasped Bethany's hand, and walked forward along the tree branch. He stepped carefully over the rough ridges of the bark. Some of the ridges were so tall he had to let go of Bethany's hand and climb over them. He was doing just that when Bethany stumbled and fell with a scream. Nick quickly turned and grasped her hand with both of his and braced himself to keep her from falling off the branch. Feeling his heart racing, he pulled her back up onto her feet. Bethany threw her arms around him and held on tightly until her breathing and heart rate returned to normal.

"Hey, be careful," said Nick, stroking her hair as she clung tightly to him.

"I'll try," she said with a weak smile. "I never have liked heights. At least not any higher than the back of a horse," she added, forcing a chuckle.

When they reached the doorway, they heard lovely humming coming from within. The sweet aroma of baking pastries greeted their nostrils. They stepped through the entrance and into the small, comfortable room. A round braided rug covered most of the floor. On the far side of the room, a little fireplace with glowing embers provided both heat and light to the circular room. By the fireplace, a well-used wingback chair awaited an occupant. Cupboards of various sizes and designs covered most of the walls. The fairy named Animara was heating water over a stove. Nick realized this was the first time since he had been in Celestia that he had seen someone cooking. All the other food he had seen and consumed was simply called forth from the air, trees, or ground in a finished and ready-for-consumption state.

"Thank you for agreeing to see us and inviting us in, Animara," said Nick, speaking to the fairy's back.

"Yes, thank you," added Bethany. "We are very pleased to be here."

The fairy continued to hum his lovely song without turning around or acknowledging their expressions of gratitude. As the fairy bustled around his quaint kitchen, Nick noticed his attire. It was different from the soft, lightweight flowing tunics the other fairies wore. He had on a long purple robe decorated with sparkling beads. The robe hung down to midcalf, revealing a white gown that reached to the floor, covering his feet. The tunic was cinched tightly around his waist with a golden belt.

As he hummed with his back still to them, Animara placed three tiny teacups on the counter of a little cabinet that stood beside the stove. Into each cup, he placed a teaspoon of honey and added some crushed peppermint leaves. When the teapot joined his humming with a whistle, he filled each cup to the brim and then used his long, thin index finger to stir them. The hot water didn't seem to bother him. Deftly picking up all three cups, he turned to face them, a warm smile on his wrinkled face.

"Tea time," he said jovially. He placed the three cups on a little table in front of his chair. Waving his hands over his head, two more chairs, identical to the first, appeared from the air and settled themselves in a semicircle facing the little fireplace. "Please, sit . . . sit," he said, motioning to the chairs.

Bethany and Nick settled into the newly arrived chairs while their host removed cranberry muffins from the oven. A napkin for each of them floated down from somewhere above them and laid itself smoothly across their laps. Animara handed both of them a teacup and a tiny plate with a muffin centered upon it. He sat himself comfortably in his chair. After wiggling into a comfortable position, the ancient fairy took a sip of his tea and a bite of his muffin before he spoke. "Let me begin by telling you how pleased I am to officially make your acquaintances. My fairies have been keeping me informed of your progress and your great work. My, my, but you both are very brave. You wear the title of legionnaire very well!"

"Thank you, Animara. It is an honor for us to be here," responded Nick.

"Now, please tell me why you have come," said Animara, taking a sip of his peppermint tea while looking at them both over the rim of his cup. He paused and smiled while keeping his eyes moving back and forth between the two unicorn riders.

"We want you to heal Hasbadana," said Nick without hesitation.

Animara choked on the tea he had sipped, and sputtered it out of his mouth. Slowly and deliberately, he lowered his teacup, placed it on the little table in front of him, picked up his napkin, and dabbed at the spilled tea. Nick and Bethany watched and waited. They did not say a word.

"My, my, I certainly did not expect such a request. That is a very unusual appeal, very unusual indeed," he finally said, looking back at them with eyes filled with both concern and fascination. "What do you mean when you say you want me to heal Hasbadana?"

Bethany spoke up. "As you know, he has taken Urijah captive."

"*Taken* Urijah?" he interrupted.

"Well, no. Actually, Urijah has given himself to Hasbadana in exchange for our safe return."

Animara nodded his tiny, grayed head. "That is better. It is important that we be precise in our language."

Nick jumped in. "We understand that Urijah gave himself willingly to save us." Animara nodded again. "But," Nick continued, "we have a plan that we think will save him."

"And this plan involves what you call 'healing' Hasbadana?"

"Yes. If Hasbadana were to be healed of his evil ways and his wicked ambitions, we're sure he would release Urijah of his own volition." Nick rushed on. "I remember when the fairies gave me the power to heal. They told me that healing the spirit was the hardest thing to do. But they did not say it was impossible."

"Impossible, no. Extremely difficult, yes," said Animara. "Especially in Hasbadana's case."

"Then there is a way?" asked Bethany, barely able to contain her excitement.

Animara looked down at his hands as they rested in his lap, holding his plate. He started humming his little melody. Nick and Bethany found themselves watching and waiting once again.

After a time, Animara looked up. "Have either of you heard the expression 'the eyes are the window to the soul'?"

Nick nodded. Bethany cocked her head to one side with a look of incomprehension on her face.

Animara directed his attention to Bethany. "Tell me, Bethany. What did you notice about Hasbadana's eyes?"

Bethany let out a long breath and slumped back in her chair. She slowly shook her head. "They're his most striking feature. I shall never forget them." She took in and released another deep breath before she continued. "They are bright red and glowing, yet they are as cold as ice. There is no depth in them, and they remain the same whether he is euphoric or irate. And his stare . . . his stare was riveting; perhaps I should say 'hypnotic.' During my weakest moments, I wasn't able to get myself to look away."

Animara pensively nodded his head. He turned to Nick. "Nicholas, you have heard Hasbadana speak in an attempt to persuade others to join him. Tell me about that, would you please?"

Nick nodded his head. When he spoke, his words came haltingly, as though he was having difficulty selecting just the right ones to use. "I've never been in the presence of anyone else like him. He can be as smooth as butter, benevolent almost, as if he has only your best interests at heart. At the same time, he is very manipulative. I nearly found myself coerced into joining him by his flattery and persuasive arguments. I listened to him recruit horses to his cause in the mists of darkness. He acted as though he empathized with their circumstances and told them he was there to help them. Yet, when I saw how he treated his army, I witnessed firsthand how cold and heartless he was. He is motivated only by a relentless drive to acquire power. He used all of those horses to obtain that end."

"Tell me, Nicholas. How was Hasbadana able to gain and maintain power over his followers?"

"First, he would use charm, then intimidation, and finally aggression to control them."

Animara listened intently to each word, occasionally nodding his head. His muffin sat on his plate with only one bite out of it. When Nick was finished with his description, Animara quietly asked, "Nicholas, what is the source of your power?"

"Love," replied Nick without hesitation.

"Then what do you suppose is the source of Hasbadana's power?"

Nick pursed his lips and shook his head. He knotted his eyebrows, searching his thoughts for an answer. "He has great power, to be sure. Yet he shows no sign of true love or even sincere empathy toward others. And when he hurts or destroys his followers, he gives no indication that he feels any remorse. He seems to be incapable of feeling any emotion at all other than self-love. Perhaps he draws all of his power by draining the love from others."

"Is there anything else you have noticed about him?"

Bethany, who had been sitting on the edge of her chair, eagerly waiting for a chance to add more to the conversation, finally spoke up. "He can lie without feeling any guilt. It's as though he has no inner voice telling him that what he is doing or saying is wrong."

Animara nodded his head solemnly. "You both have described Hasbadana very well, and therein lays the difficulty of what you have come to ask me to do. Healing him will be extremely difficult because he will have no desire to be healed, not sensing that there is anything wrong with his view of the world and his approach to navigating around it. To him, others exist only to meet his needs and to help him achieve his goals. In his mind, that is as it should be." Animara reached for his teacup and stirred the warm tea with his finger as he gazed at the glowing embers in the fireplace.

The ancient fairy sat pensively, looking at the fire but not really seeing it. Finally he turned his head and looked back at Nick and Bethany. He removed his finger from the teacup and waved his hand toward them. "Please, please, eat. Eat while I think." That being said, he turned his gaze back to the little fire and started humming again, his finger returning to the task of stirring his tea.

Bethany and Nick each took a bite of their muffin. As it melted in their mouths, they were filled with a strong sensation of hunger and both quickly finished the treat and gulped down their tea. Just as Nick looked around for more, new muffins appeared on both of their little plates and the teacups started steaming with a fresh brew. They ate until they felt satisfied.

Once they finished eating, Nick began examining the room in which they sat. It was a very comfortable and cozy room, so much so that it was easy for him to forget that he had been shrunk to just eight inches in order to fit inside of it. His attention was drawn to the many cupboards that lined the walls. They were all different shapes, sizes, and colors. Some sat on the floor; others hung at different heights on the walls. Each cupboard door was securely shut, though whether they were locked, Nick could not tell.

He looked upward and noticed, for the first time, the beautiful wooden beams that decorated and supported the ceiling. From many of these beams, banners of sparkling fabric hung down. Each banner was approximately four feet in length and was decorated with stars in the shape of constellations. The stars sparkled with a light all their own. As was true with all of the night stars in Celestia, none of the constellations were familiar to Nick.

The young unicorn rider looked down at the floor. Most of it, as he had noticed earlier, was covered with a circular braided rug. But, as he looked closer, he noticed, for the first time, that the fabrics in the rug, though subtle, were actually changing color. A band that a moment before had been purple, was now a deep shade of blue. The red was now orange. It was as though each strand in the braid was moving through all of the colors of the rainbow. "Bethany," he whispered, "look at the rug."

Bethany looked down and her eyes widened. She smiled with delight as she watched it change from one hue to another. The two of them became transfixed as they watched the colors change. They were not aware of the passage of time.

At last, the humming stopped and Animara turned back to face them. "You are right, Nicholas, when you say that this is a sickness of the spirit. However, I sense that it is more than that. The unicorn brain, like that of the fairies, and the humans for that matter, is made up of two halves. Each half is assigned its own tasks, some tasks being assigned to the right side of the brain; others to the left. I believe that both sides of Hasbadana's brain are competing for the same functions. This creates a continuous flow of negative energy between the two sides of his brain. Hasbadana's brain is filled with constant conflict and confusion with the result that he cannot respond to reason the way we would. As a consequence, he is incapable of feeling any emotion, and his sole motivation is to achieve his own desires without regard to what he must do or who he must hurt to get what he wants." He paused and shook his head. "This will be our most challenging task yet. Oh yes, far more challenging even than restoring life. We will have to heal both the damage to his brain and the weaknesses of his spirit. We have never attempted to undertake such a demanding healing."

Nick leaned forward in his chair, his hands grasped together. "But you will do it?"

Animara looked intently into Nick's eyes for a few moments as if trying to measure the depth of Nick's sincerity and commitment. Seeing something essential in the deepest part of the young man's soul, he answered softly, "I will try."

Chapter 18

Bucephalus

Deep within the dark halls of Valhalla, Hasbadana's corroded and crumbling castle, Urijah stood in silence. Rusted chains encircled his body, running from one sparkling leg to another, over his back and around his neck. Burnt orange marks from the rusted metal stained the white hairs of his glistening coat, though nothing could dull the shine. Moving was so difficult that Urijah was forced to spend his days with his head down, resting his iridescent horn on the cold stone floor.

He spent most days alone in the silence of his damp, dark cell, his glowing body providing the only light. But today, the door to his cubicle opened, and the noise from the rusting metal hinges created a shrill, screeching sound. Urijah lifted his head. Entering through the doorway was his warden, Hasbadana.

Hasbadana avoided coming to see Urijah, as it pained him to be in the presence of so much light. *Better to stay away*, he told himself. What had drawn him here today, he could not say. But there he stood, facing his nemesis.

"My, my, but you are looking fine today, *Lord* Urijah," he said with a sardonic smile on his black, angular face.

"Hello, Hasbadana," responded Urijah gently.

"Have you been missing me?"

"As a matter of fact, I have. It is rather lonely down here."

Hasbadana, followed by his guards who stood behind him, burst into raucous laughter. "Well," Hasbadana said when he had his voice back, "let me brighten your day!" He chuckled again.

Urijah stood patiently, waiting for the purpose of this visit to be revealed.

Hasbadana stepped farther into the room. Suddenly, he turned and commanded his guards to leave and close the door behind them.

"Are you certain, Master?" said one, concern reflected in his red eyes.

"I said, GO!" bellowed the ruler of the Dark Kingdom.

The two guards whirled on their haunches and left the cell. The door slammed shut behind them.

Hasbadana walked slowly around the perimeter of the cubicle, staying close to the stone walls. He kept his eyes on his prisoner, carefully checking to make sure that all of the chains were secure.

"You need not fear, Hasbadana. I have not tried to escape. Nor will I," said Urijah as he tracked the dark lord's footsteps around the room.

"Ha, the noble and great martyr."

"Not a martyr. I am here by my own choice."

"Choice! Your fatuous infatuation with agency fills me with both hilarity and nausea. Look where it has gotten you now! You are under my control. You are now the Lord of all you survey . . . this lovely cell!" Hasbadana laughed aloud. "You can't even use your powers to communicate with your thoughts, as I have created a barrier that prevents you from doing so."

"Yes, Hasbadana, I have noticed as much," responded Urijah patiently. "Why do you have such animosity toward my belief that we all should be given the freedom to choose? Animals and humans both must be free to act and not to be acted upon."

Hasbadana let out a derisive snort and tossed his head. Urijah ignored it and continued. "Hasbadana, we have never used force as our form of governance. We teach correct principles with love and let the animals and humans govern themselves."

"Ha! And just how has that method worked out for you?"

Urijah slowly nodded his head. "You are right on that point. The animals have done quite well, but it is true that many of the humans have not chosen as wisely."

"And we animals are often the victims of their poor choices," roared Hasbadana.

"Again, I cannot argue with you. But most of the humans are wonderful. They do not deserve to be punished for the mistakes of the few."

Hasbadana shook his head sharply from side to side, his thick black forelock bouncing from one side of his steel-black horn to the other. "Enough!" he yelled. "I do not need more of your proselytizing. Those 'few,' as you call them, have created great misery for the animals. And just look at you! Here you stand in chains because of your convictions when it is your true destiny to run across the earth and the heavens, free of saddle and bridle." Hasbadana paused, shook his head, and said: "Tsk, tsk, such a sad state of affairs to see what you have become."

When the giant unicorn completed his circle of the room, he stopped and faced Urijah. "Tell me, Lord Urijah, how much do you know about me? Do you know who I was in mortality?"

Urijah looked at Hasbadana calmly but didn't respond. He knew the question was rhetorical. He allowed Hasbadana to continue uninterrupted.

"I was the greatest horse that ever lived. I was the legendary Bucephalus!" he said, his voice rising. He paused for a moment and stared at Urijah, waiting for the look of awe and respect he was accustomed to receiving but, in this instance, didn't really expect to be forthcoming.

Urijah smiled at him warmly. "Tell me about your earth life, Hasbadana," preferring to use his unicorn name.

Hasbadana looked up at the ceiling, picturing his earth life in his mind. Finally he spoke. "I was foaled in a land called Thessaly. It was a land famous for its magnificent horses. For twelve years of my life, I ran with the other horses across the grassy plains. All the mares followed me. The other stallions feared me . . . as rightfully they should." He sneered indignantly. "But when I turned twelve, a group of humans captured me and tore me away from my herd, my mares, and my foals." His voice rose in anger and he snorted loudly before continuing. "They took me on a long journey to a northern country by the name of Macedonia. It was their intention to sell me to the ruler of that kingdom named Phillip II."

He snapped his head around and glared at Urijah. "Thirteen talents! Thirteen talents! That is what they asked for my life. As though any price was enough for a horse such as me!" Hasbadana snorted loudly again, tossed his head, and stomped a hoof.

He took a deep breath to calm himself before continuing. "The men placed me in an enclosure with the intention of showing me to the king. But I was frightened. The men and their shadows, caused by the blazing sun, surrounded me." He paused and tilted his head to one side as he added, "Yes, it is true, I was once afraid of shadows." A deep whinny-like chuckle arose from his throat.

"But, I digress. In any case, finding myself in this threatening situation, I put all of my enormous and enviable strength toward fighting them. As you might have anticipated, I emerged the victor. I refused to let anyone ride me. After awhile I thought I had bested them all. The king wanted nothing to do with a horse as wild as me. He feared me and said I could never be ridden. He was right, you know. No one could ever have ridden me unless I desired it to be so.

"But then, something unusual happened. A young boy the same age as I—just twelve years of age—walked quietly up to me. He gently took hold of my bridle and turned me until I was facing the sun. No longer was I frightened by the shadows, as I could no longer see them. I snorted and pawed the ground, but the boy stood quietly and calmly beside me. I planted my feet on the ground and looked the lad in the eyes. He had the kindest eyes I had ever seen on a human. He smiled and rubbed my forehead. 'My, you have a big, beautiful head. I think I shall call you Bucephalus,' he said as he continued rubbing me. I felt calmness permeate my body. Slowly he moved to my side, removed his cloak, and threw it over my back. I snorted but remained standing. In the blink of an eye, he clasped my mane and swung up onto my back. I reared but once, before he sent me forward. We ran and ran until the two of us were one." Hasbadana paused and looked down at the floor. "That Nicholas of yours reminds me of my Alexander."

"Alexander the Great," added Urijah by way of encouragement.

"Yes, Alexander the Great, born in Greece on the same day as me in the year 356 BC. He was the son of King Philip II. When we returned from our gallop, the king gave me to him and declared that Macedonia was too small a kingdom for such as the two of us."

"And that was true, was it not?" prodded Urijah.

"Of course it was true! The name Bucephalus, which means ox-head, for my head was as broad as a bull's, became known and justifiably feared all over the land. For sixteen years, Alexander and I rode into battle. For sixteen years I carried him safely home. Before we were done, we had conquered the entire Persian Empire. We were never defeated. My Alexander, son of a king and tutored by Aristotle himself, became the ruler of this enormous kingdom, you know."

"And you were killed in battle?"

Hasbadana reared, pawing the air, and let out a loud, shrill neigh. His guards burst through the door, fearing their leader was in danger. Hasbadana lowered his front hooves to the floor and whirled around to face the two dark unicorns. Directing his anger to them he bellowed, "Be gone, you imbeciles!"

"We're sorry, master. Forgive us, we only meant to help . . ."

"Be gone!" Hasbadana roared again. The two guards dashed out as quickly as they had entered, shutting the door loudly behind them.

With contrived calmness, Hasbadana turned back to Urijah. "That is a lie, though I can understand why it was spread. It was one of those necessary, vital lies that has the ability to inspire others to do what you want them to do. Truth and falsehood are, after all, arbitrary terms. But, for your information, I was never defeated in battle. I stood up to men, horses, and even the elephants of India at the battle by the Hydaspes River. I leaped over their heads, always carrying my beloved Alexander to safety. And what did I get in return? Do you want to know the truth?" Hasbadana paused as he narrowed his eyes and glared at Urijah. "I was put out to pasture! Me! The great Bucephalus, the greatest horse that has ever galloped across the face of the earth, was put out to pasture!" he said, his voice rising in a crescendo.

"You had earned a rest," said Urijah. The Lord of Celestia ached for what was once a noble and great horse and an even greater unicorn. The pain in Hasbadana's heart was palpable.

"I didn't need a rest! I didn't want a rest! I wanted Alexander the Great and his celebrated horse, Bucephalus, to continue conquering the world throughout all eternity. I was still as swift as an eagle and as strong as the ox for whom I was named. He had no right to just cast me off!" Hasbadana's red eyes glowed brightly and his sides heaved. He snorted and pawed the stone floor, the anger within him needing a release. He raised his head and addressed Alexander as though he were in the room. "You tell me that you need me, then you cast me off. No, no, your apologies are too late. Your murals and paintings, your cities named after me, even your sculptures, they all mean nothing to me. Nothing!"

"Hasbadana," whispered Urijah. "You misunderstand."

Hasbadana turned back toward Urijah. The lord of the Dark Kingdom lifted his head with a start and blinked his eyes several times as though he was surprised to see Urijah there. He shook his head and brought himself back to the present time. "No, I *do* understand!" the lord of the Dark Kingdom shouted. "It is *you* who misunderstands. Throughout time, humans have abused us. They have used us and cast us away. This agency that means so much to you . . . it was denied to me! Yes, where was my freedom to choose how I would live my life? He took it away."

"He loved you." Sorrow filled Urijah's heart as he bore the pain that Hasbadana was carrying with him. All of this ache and anger was the result of a perceived offense and a failure to forgive.

"Don't say it. It is beneath you to lie for him." Hasbadana turned his back on Urijah. When he spoke again, it was barely a whisper. "I once thought I knew what love was, but no more. Love does not turn you away." He shook his head. "There is no such thing as love, Urijah. It is a fantasy." Hasbadana turned sharply back to face Urijah. "Look at you. If there was such a thing as the 'power of love' as you always say, you would not be shackled here in chains, cowering before me."

"Ah, but that is where you are wrong. I am here precisely because of love." Hasbadana snorted his disgust, but Urijah ignored him and continued. "I have chosen to lay down my life for that of the humans you captured. I traded my enslavement for their freedom. It was because of love that I did that."

"Then you are a bigger fool than I thought."

"Cast your burdens upon me. I will carry them for you," said Urijah in a whisper.

"You carry my burdens? You *are* my burden!" An evil laugh arose from deep within his chest. "But no more! You have left your starry pavilion and now get to experience the feelings of rejection and loneliness that you forced upon me!"

"No pain or sorrow, no loss or failure, is beyond my comprehension and my compassion. I have suffered them all," responded Urijah, calmly.

"Not for me, you haven't!" Hasbadana whirled around. "Open!" he commanded the door, which immediately obeyed. He left the room, determined to never come back.

Chapter 19

Animara's Plan

After their initial meeting with Animara, Nick and Bethany were sent away so that Animara could be alone to study and ponder the problem of healing Hasbadana. Every book the patriarch of the fairies had collected throughout his extremely long life was opened and pored over by the ancient little healer. All day and into the night he studied, trying to find a solution.

It was still dark when the fairies came to awaken Nick and Lazari. Nick sat up quickly in his bed when he heard his name being called in the high-pitched voice of Gidoni. "Master Nicholas, Master Nicholas," said Gidoni as he, and the two fairies with him, kept a safe distance away from the rider's flailing arms. "Animara has emerged from his home and would like to have an audience with you immediately."

"Animara? He wants to see me?" Nick said, his voice sounding groggy.

"Yes. He desires to see you immediately."

Nick threw back his down-filled comforter and leapt out of bed. "Lazari? Did you hear that? Animara is ready to see us."

Lazari stepped through the archway that separated his stall from Nick's room. He stretched both of his front legs forward and lowered his shoulders down until his elbows nearly touched the ground. He stood back up and shook the straw from his body and long, thick mane and tail. "Well, we mustn't keep him waiting," he said with a smile.

Nick swung up onto Lazari's back and ducked his head as the unicorn dashed out the cottage door. They followed Gidoni as the pale green fairy and his colorful companions darted over and around the trees and bushes. The moon was still bathing the land with white and causing the three fairies to sparkle like bright, colorful stars shooting through the air.

Animara's magical tree house was on the far side of Celestia. It took them quite awhile to get there, even with Lazari running his fastest. When the stands of fir and pine were replaced by the forest of deciduous trees, Nick knew they were getting close. The deciduous forest they were passing through was populated with trees that shed all of their leaves and flower petals each night. The bare branches of the trees reminded Nick of the skeleton trees in the Dark Kingdom with one significant difference. The exposed branches and trunks of these trees glowed as they reflected the light of the moon. The petals that covered the ground continued to twinkle as they filled the air with a dizzying perfume.

They galloped up the hill between the tall, white aspen. The entire hillside, white and green when they first saw it, was now completely white, and the giant flowers and huge tree trunks nearly disappeared in the light of the moon.

Suddenly, Lazari's head came up, his ears pricked forward, and he came to a sudden stop. Ahead of them, in the center of the clearing at the top of the hill, stood Animara's tree. Nick remembered how wondrous it had been in the daylight with its fluorescent green leaves and the flowers that were white with bright pink centers. He remembered how the blossoms opened and shut their petals, making the tree appear to be in constant motion. Tonight, Nick and Lazari both stared up at the magical tree, their eyes wide with fascination. If it could be possible, the tree was even more beautiful at night under the light of the moon. The flower petals continued their performance, but as each opened, the pink centers twinkled like little lights. The gnarled trunk and exposed roots of the tree radiated a purple light. Though reminiscent of the painting "Starry Night," the entire picture was something beyond anyone's imagination, even beyond something that the artist Vincent Van Gogh could have imagined.

Nick slipped off Lazari's back and, with his hand on his unicorn's strong shoulder, stepped forward toward the tree. At the base of the enormous plant, they stopped and looked up through the twisted branches. Nick turned around to find Gidoni, anticipating the magic that would carry him to the top.

"We are waiting for Bethany and Shema. Junia was sent to fetch them. I'm sure they will be here in a moment," said Gidoni in response to Nick's beseeching expression.

Sure enough, within a few minutes, Junia fluttered into the clearing with Shema and Bethany right behind. Bethany jumped off her unicorn before the mare had even come to a halt and ran up to Nick. "We came as quickly as we could," she said while trying to catch her breath. "Does he have a solution for us?"

"I don't know," answered Nick, reaching for her outstretched hand. "We just arrived here ourselves."

Like the last time they came to visit Animara, Gidoni flew over their heads in a figure eight pattern while chanting the unusual words from the fairy language. Once his pattern was complete, he headed for the highest branches of the tree. Nick and Bethany were instantly carried through the air, this time knowing what to expect. Again, they were placed down on the wide branch that served as a walkway to Animara's home.

Suddenly, dozens of fairies appeared from the branches around them as though they had been awaiting their arrival. As they had done before, the fairies flew over their heads, singing a beautiful song in the ancient language of the fairies. With a sizzling and popping sound, Nick and Bethany were, once again, reduced to the size of a fairy.

The two tiny humans stepped up to the door and knocked. Silently, it opened for them. Just as before, Animara was busy taking muffins out of the oven. A teapot sang on the stove, and peppermint leaves lingered in the bottom of three teacups awaiting the splash of hot water. Three wingback chairs waited for occupants in front of the crackling fire. Animara, without looking at them, waved a hand toward the chairs. "Sit, sit," he said over his shoulder.

Bethany and Nick each took a chair and waited. Animara hummed a song as he removed the muffins from the pan and artfully arranged them on a plate. He placed the plate on a delicate tea cart, added the teacups and the pot of hot water, and pushed it over to their chairs. "Please, help yourselves," he said with a smile on his face and a twinkle in his eye.

"Thank you, Animara," said Bethany politely as she helped herself to the peppermint tea and cranberry muffins.

Nick, on the other hand, was bursting with curiosity, and he didn't know how much longer he could wait for Animara to get to the point. *Patience*, he kept thinking. He hurriedly placed a muffin on a plate, poured some hot water into a teacup, and leaned against the soft back of the chair.

Slowly and deliberately, Animara served himself, still humming his little song in the high soprano range of his voice. When he sat down, he stopped humming and started stirring his tea with his finger. Eventually, he looked up at Nick and Bethany.

"I hope you will forgive me for summoning you in the middle of the night. I realize you must be very tired after your latest assignment to and from the Dark Kingdom."

Nick shook his head. "Do not worry a bit. We are eager to hear what you have to say."

"Tell me," the ancient fairy began, "about your relationship with Nebbish, the lord of the Underground Kingdom of Mantelia."

"What do you want to know?" asked Nick.

"Did you leave him on good terms?"

"Yes."

"Very good terms?" Animara quizzed further.

"Yes, very good. We were able to heal their newborn Rodorix babies."

"Do you feel he would be willing to help you?"

"The Rodorix said they would help me whenever I was in need. They even gave me instructions on how to contact them if I needed their assistance. Why?"

Animara nodded thoughtfully. "That is good. That is very good."

"What are you thinking, Animara?" asked Nick again.

"I am thinking we might need them to play an integral part in rescuing Urijah and helping us heal Hasbadana."

Nick and Bethany exchanged glances. Nick turned back to Animara. "How would they do that?"

"Tell me, Nicholas and Bethany, have either of you heard of amethyst?"

Bethany responded first. "Are you referring to the lovely purple crystals?"

"I am, indeed. You see, the ethereal purple hues are so much more than beautiful. Nature itself invested this crystal with several therapeutic properties as the crystals were formed. At the time of their creation, amethyst crystals absorbed the earth's energy. As a result, they are filled with magical powers."

"What kind of magical powers?" asked Bethany.

"Well, my dear," he paused long enough to take a sip of his tea before continuing, "of particular interest to us at this time is their power to stimulate the right side of the brain. As they do this, traumas of the past are replaced with a feeling of peace. They have a tremendous ability to absorb negative energy. And also of great help to us, amethyst crystals help an animal trust in the power of love."

"That is just what we need," said Nick with excitement. "But what does that have to do with the Rodorix?"

"If you think they will cooperate with us, I will tell you."

The circular braided rug that covered the floor changed its colors slowly, causing the mood of the room to change with it. When it was dominated by blues and purples, the room felt peaceful and calm. When the colors were reds and oranges, Animara's home felt like it was filled with energy. That was how it felt now.

Nick looked up at the ancient fairy, a smile stretching across the young man's face. "They will help us. I know they will."

Animara smiled warmly as he nodded his head. "Then, perhaps, you would like to hear my proposal?" he asked rhetorically.

Nick and Bethany both slid to the front of their wingback chairs and leaned forward, eager to hear what this most ancient of all fairies had devised for a plan. The colors on the braided rug changed to shades of blue and purple. Animara motioned with his thin, frail hand to the rug. Bethany and Nick followed the motion with their eyes. "What are you feeling now?" he asked in his high-pitched voice.

"I feel very peaceful," responded Bethany.

"As do I," answered Nick.

"If the Rodorix will help us, I would like us to craft a room that not only feels peaceful, but actually has the power to create peace within a soul . . . Hasbadana's soul."

Bethany opened her eyes wide. "With amethyst?"

Animara smiled and winked at Bethany. "Precisely, my dear. With amethyst."

Nick looked back and forth between these two, who seemed to be on the same wavelength. He wasn't sure that he completely understood. "You think amethyst has the power to heal Hasbadana?" he asked incredulously.

"That I do. But it will be necessary to completely surround him with the crystals."

"How will we ever do that?" asked Nick, skepticism still filling his heart and mind.

"That is where the Rodorix come in. They are able to mine all of the crystals underground. We will need them to find the amethyst and bring it to an underground chamber. We will call upon the power of the unicorns to command the elements to line the walls, floor, and ceiling, thus creating a room entirely covered with the lovely lavender crystals."

"But once that is complete, how do we get Hasbadana into it?" asked Bethany.

"It may take some clever convincing, to be sure, but I am confident that we can appeal to his ego," responded Animara with a smile.

"Appeal to his ego? In what way?" asked Nick.

"We must convince him that the Rodorix have created a room that will make him more powerful."

"But we have made a pledge to be honest," said Bethany and Nick simultaneously.

"Exactly! What could be more powerful than to have the anger and bitterness removed and replaced by love?"

Nick and Bethany looked at one another. When their eyes met, each could see the sparkle in the other's eyes.

Slowly, Nick turned back to Animara. "Do you really think this will work?" he asked again, seeking reassurance.

Animara took a deep breath and slowly exhaled. "I admit that we have never attempted such a thing. But it seems to me that it will work. However, I must concede that I cannot be sure of the effects the amethyst will have on Hasbadana."

"Well, I think it's certainly worth a try," said Bethany as she leapt to her feet. She crossed over to the ancient fairy and gave him a hug. As she did so, Animara looked over her shoulder at Nick and smiled broadly.

chapter 20

The Proposal

Looking around at Lazari, Shema, Bethany, and Mastis, Nick took a deep breath. Letting the air out with a loud rushing sound, he raised his arm and stabbed the ground with the golden spade that Mastis had called forth. Setting the spade down, he reached around and grasped the small bag that hung at his hip. He inserted his hand into the pouch and let his fingers wiggle through the clover. At last, they made contact with something smooth and hard nestled in the bottom of the bag. Nick clutched the item he was feeling and brought it out. He placed it in the palm of his other hand and held it up for all to see. In the rider's open palm rested a beautiful lavender crystal. The stone was about two inches long and one-half inch wide. It sparkled as its smooth angles reflected the light of the sun.

"That is beautiful, just beautiful," said Shema.

"Yes, what is that?" asked Bethany.

Mastis and Lazari stood silently, having read Nick's thoughts beforehand.

"Nehor gave me this crystal and told me that if I placed it in the ground, he would know that I needed his help," responded Nick.

Lazari nodded his head, and his long black forelock bounced from one side of his amber-colored horn to the other. "Well, let's do it then."

"Okay . . . here goes," said Nick as he turned his hand and let the lavender crystal fall into the hole he had made with the golden spade. As soon as it hit the dirt in the bottom of the hole, the crystal started to glow, sending up a straight, narrow, violet beam of light high into the air. The dirt around it started to melt, and the hole got bigger and deeper. Suddenly, the ground started to shake.

"Oh, dear me, dear me," said Shema as she backed away. Nick leaped to his feet and scrambled backward to stand beside Lazari as the depression became a large sinkhole, several feet across.

The members of the Legion of the Unicorn watched; the ground stopped shaking and all became still. As they waited, the gentle music of Celestia filled the air. Nick was surprised at the anxiety he felt. *What if Nehor doesn't come?* he said in his thoughts to his unicorn.

I have faith in him. He will keep his word, responded Lazari

Their patience was rewarded when Nehor appeared in the hole. His pointed nose and luminescent whiskers appeared first. He rose higher until he placed his elbows on the ground at the edge of the hole and rested his chin on his narrow front paws. With a crooked smile on his face, he winked at Nick and said, "I knew you'd be calling."

"Hi, Nehor," said Nick and Bethany at once. Nick's anxiety was immediately replaced with an overwhelming sense of relief.

"And just who are these unicorns with you?" asked their Rodorix friend.

"Oh, forgive me. This is my unicorn partner, Lazari," Nick said, patting the dark bay gelding's neck. Then he motioned to the unicorns beside him with a sweep of his arm. "And this is Shema, Bethany's partner, and our savior and mentor, Mastis."

"Very pleased to make your acquaintance," said Nehor.

"And we feel the same," responded Mastis with a deep bow.

"Now, no more chitchat. Let's get to the reason you summoned me," said Nehor, dropping his paws and climbing out of the hole. His odd-shaped body moved with surprising gracefulness across the surface of Celestia, and his tail seemed even longer than Nick had remembered as it followed him out of the hole. "Tell me, Nicholas, what is on your mind?"

"Do you know the ancient fairy Animara?"

"I know of his reputation. We considered contacting him to heal our infants. However, you dropped in first," he said with a laugh.

Nick smiled at the Rodorix's joke. "Well, he has come up with a plan to heal Hasbadana."

Nehor choked and sputtered. "Heal Hasbadana?" *Cough . . . cough . . .* "Impossible! You say this was Animara's idea?"

"Well," responded Nick softly. "I asked him to do it."

"The fairy must have become mad in his old age to even consider such a thing."

Mastis stepped forward. "My new friend, Nehor, I know this sounds implausible, but we and the members of the Council of the Twelve Ancients, who are governing in Urijah's absence, believe the ancient fairy has come up with a plan that just might work."

Lazari stepped up beside Mastis. "But it would all depend upon the Rodorix's willingness to help."

Nehor looked back and forth between Nick and the two unicorns. He narrowed his eyes, tilted his head to one side, and slowly said, "And just what is this plan?"

Bethany, unable to contain her excitement, jumped in. "Oh, Nehor, it is a wonderful plan."

Nehor looked over at her and raised his eyebrows. Skeptical though he was, he nodded his head, encouraging her to continue.

"Animara wants to call upon the power of the amethyst to draw all of the negative feelings out of Hasbadana and replace them with love," she said, excitement still evident in her voice.

"Amethyst?" the pointy-nosed Rodorix answered. "Amethyst?" he said again softly to himself. He looked down at his small front paws now resting on his large belly. His tail swished from side to side and his claws started drumming. "Amethyst. I wonder . . ." he said as he scratched his head with his claws while deep in thought. The legion members waited patiently.

Nehor looked up. "Tell me more about this plan. There must be more."

"Yes," Nick responded. "With your help finding and mining the amethyst and our ability to command the elements, we want to create a chamber of amethyst and then convince Hasbadana to enter into it."

Nehor snorted and rolled his eyes. "Ah . . . I knew there was a catch. Building such a chamber would be a herculean task in and of itself, but just how do you propose we get him into this room if we can even get it built? He isn't known for being cooperative, you know."

At this moment, a large Clydesdale unicorn stepped out of the woods that surrounded Nick and Lazari's clearing. "That is where I come in," said Portlas with a smile.

Nick and Bethany snapped their heads around. "Portlas? What do you mean?" asked Nick.

"The council has asked me to return to the Dark Kingdom to convince Hasbadana to go to the Underground Kingdom and enter the amethyst chamber. He already suspects that my conversion to the light is tenuous, so the council believes I will be able to convince Hasbadana to come to the Underground Kingdom and enter the amethyst chamber."

Mastis nodded his head and smiled at Portlas. "That is an excellent idea. You know his ways and have been able to resist his powers of persuasion in the past. I think you are the perfect choice."

Bethany stepped up to the huge unicorn and stroked the white blaze that ran down the center of his large head. "Thank you, Portlas. You are very brave."

Portlas dropped his head and nuzzled her cheek. With a smile he added, "Not really; it scares me to death. But I have learned that I must replace my fears with love." He looked up and winked at Lazari, who often said those very words.

"Excuse me for interrupting this love fest," said Nehor as he cleared his throat. "But just how will you convince him to come to the Underground Kingdom?"

"I will appeal to his ego and his never-ceasing search for additional victims from whom he can draw power. I will tell him the Rodorix have built a chamber that can help him become even more dominant. This will not be a lie, for if we can heal him, he *will* be more powerful," responded Portlas.

"Will he believe you?" asked Nehor skeptically.

"Hasbadana is always seeking more ways to increase his authority and enlarge his kingdom. He has often expressed a desire to expand his sphere of influence to the Underground Kingdom as a source of more subjects over whom he can have dominion. When I offer him an opportunity to go to the

Underground Kingdom, I believe he will accept my offer with enthusiasm."

"And what if it doesn't work? What if the amethyst is not powerful enough to heal him? Then we have to deal with Hasbadana in our own kingdom," said Nehor, genuine concern expressed in his eyes and across his face. "How will we control him once he is released underground?"

Mastis spoke up. "We will have the entire Legion of the Unicorn there to assist and protect you if you will allow us to enter your kingdom."

Nehor frowned and his eyebrows knotted as he carefully considered all the information he had just been given. "As you must know, I cannot make such a decision on my own. I will need to present this to Nebbish, the lord of the Underground Kingdom. It will be up to him to make the final decision. I cannot even hazard a guess as to what his response will be."

The music that flowed softly through the air was suddenly broken into several pieces as the notes split apart and seemed to fall to the ground like tinkling brass. It was replaced by the whirring and whistling sound of hundreds of tiny wings as all of the fairies of Celestia, with Animara in the lead, flew into the clearing.

"Animara!" exclaimed Mastis, before bowing to the ground. The other legion members followed his lead. *Animara has not left his home for centuries*, he whispered in his thoughts to Nick and Lazari.

Animara acknowledged Mastis and the others with a curt bow of his head. His wings fluttered quickly, creating a blur of colored light as he held himself suspended in the air before them. Directing his comments to Nehor, he said in his tiny, shrill voice, "May I be permitted to accompany you to meet with Nebbish? I would like to present him with the plan myself."

Nehor stammered, "Why, uh, well . . . yes, I don't see why not. I am sure Nebbish would be honored to have an audience with you."

Gidoni and Junia flew up beside Animara. "Are you sure you feel able to do this, Animara?" asked Junia, clearly concerned for her leader's welfare.

Animara brushed off the inquiry with a wave of his tiny hand. "Of course I feel able to do this. I haven't felt so energized in centuries!" He patted her kindly on her shoulder and smiled, a sign that he appreciated her concern. He turned back to Nehor. "I'll follow you. And don't think I can't keep up, young man," he said with a chuckle.

Nehor disappeared into the hole and Animara flew down after him. Soft melodies once again filled the air of Celestia.

****

A day and a night and a day passed, and the hole in the ground remained empty and lifeless. Nick, Bethany, and their unicorns kept a careful watch, waiting for the return of Animara and Nehor. Mastis was sent on a mission to the earth to help an injured animal—their work needed to carry on, after all. Every few hours Nick heard Mastis speak to him in his thoughts: *Any word?*

The answer was always the same: *Not yet.*

During the night, they took turns sleeping. When it was Nick's turn to keep watch, he sat on the grass, his back propped against Lazari's shoulder. He rested his head against the unicorn's dark withers and stared up at the always-full moon. He could feel the love swell within him until he felt his heart would burst.

I love you, too, he heard Lazari say in his thoughts.

I thought you were asleep, answered Nick.

Just resting. I'm too excited and anxious to sleep.

I was just thinking about all the power you give me, thought Nick.

Yes, I heard you. You, also, are the source of much of my power. However, I sense there is a young lady sleeping beside us that provides you with a lot of power as well.

Nick reached around and slapped his unicorn's neck. *Okay, you're right.* Nick chuckled softly. Immediately he returned to his contemplative state of mind. *But my increased ability to love others has only increased my love for you*, he thought with a smile. *I have learned that love is infinite. I once thought that love was like a pie. A portion of it was for me and the rest was for everyone else. If someone received a larger piece of the pie, then that would mean less for me. Now I know that love begets love, and there is no end to its power and influence. That is why I can now be truly happy for someone else's success. That simply adds to the love for all of us.*

Lazari turned his neck and placed his muzzle on Nick's crossed leg. *I understand what you are saying. Love has the ability to increase exponentially.*

Nick reached up and rubbed Lazari's soft ears as he continued to stare up at the moon. *Yes, that is exactly what I mean.*

****

While the unicorns and their riders rested above, deep beneath the surface of Celestia, Nehor and Animara were meeting with Nebbish in his sparkling red chambers. During the meeting, Animara carefully outlined every detail of his plan. Now they were silently waiting while Nebbish paced back and forth in front of them. Occasionally Nebbish stopped, faced them, and opened his mouth as though ready to ask a question. But each time, he snapped his mouth shut, shook his head, and returned to his thoughts and his pacing. The food that was brought into the ruby-red crystal room through the glistening white doors remained untouched.

Nebbish stepped back up onto his dais and slouched down into his chair. His face wore a scowl. His fingers drummed out an uneven rhythm on the arms of his throne. "Aside from the obviously desirable outcome of freeing Urijah, tell me again just why I should do this. Why should I risk the safety of my kingdom?"

Animara flew forward. "I understand why you see this as a risk because it is out of the common course of events for you and your animals. In addition, you have, up to this point, been able to remain neutral between the forces of light and darkness. Sadly, your ability to remain neutral will not last forever. You must realize that there exists an ever-growing danger that Hasbadana will turn on your kingdom to satisfy his own desires. It would be far better to have him come here under the controlled circumstances that we propose and with the guardianship of the Legion of the Unicorn than for you to have to face a surprise attack alone."

"You really believe there is a possibility that he will try to conquer the Underground Kingdom on his own?"

"He has to gain strength and power from somewhere. His attempts at earth have been unsuccessful thus far. I do not think he will be satisfied with failure. Nor do I believe he has abandoned his plans for human and animal domination. You must also remember that he would not attack you alone. He has an entire army of dark unicorns that do his bidding. They would be the ones you would have to face."

"When might this take place?" asked Nebbish, his pointed claws curling into fists and resting firmly on the arms of his elegant red throne.

"I have no way of knowing. Eternity is a very long time, my lord. But unless we find a way to heal Hasbadana, I do not see that he has any other recourse. To gain the supremacy he desires, he will have to seek to take power from you and your kingdom."

Nebbish stood once again and returned to his pacing. Animara flew back and fluttered in the air beside Nehor. Patience was a virtue that Animara had developed well, and he was willing to let this contemplative leader take all the time he needed.

Finally, Nebbish returned to his throne. This time, however, his posture was stiff and erect. He held out his paws with the palms down. On each paw was a gold ring with a large lavender stone set in the middle. "You see, my friends, I understand the power of the amethyst," he said with a smile. "I have decided to grant your request. But I hope you realize how difficult a task you are asking us to undertake. Amethyst is not easy to find, and when we do find it, we can't use all of it. Only the purest, most flawless crystals have the qualities you seek. Stones that have dark flecks or clouds, which we call 'inclusions,' will block the radiation of energy. We will need to call upon not only the Rodorix but all of the underground animals to work together to find the perfect amethyst crystals."

Nehor stepped forward. His voice rose with excitement. "Then let us begin immediately. I will organize work teams, each with their own commanders. We will divide up the map," he said, motioning to the white doors that contained the carving of the Underground Kingdom, "and send the teams out to find the amethyst."

Nebbish nodded. "Yes, I see no reason to delay. Tell me, Nehor, since you have had more time to consider this than I have, where would you suggest we build the healing chamber?"

"Right beneath Valhalla," said Nehor with confidence.

Animara smiled and bowed to Nebbish before flying out of the Underground Lord's chamber. He had wonderful news to deliver to those waiting above.

chapter 21

executing the plan

With Nehor as his guide, Animara dashed through the labyrinth of tunnels to return to Celestia. Nick and Bethany were eagerly awaiting his return right where he had left them. At the receipt of the ancient fairy's good news, Nick sent a message to Mastis: *Nebbish has consented!*

Nick received an immediate response in his thoughts. *That is wonderful. I will be returning shortly.*

After guiding Animara to the sinkhole, Nehor set to work straightaway organizing the Rodorix, moles, voles, lemmings, and all the other underground animals into teams of miners. Each team was carefully instructed in the fine art of mining amethyst. Only the purest specimens were to be brought back to the chamber.

Nehor guided one group through the maze of tunnels until he felt confident they were right beneath Hasbadana's crumbling castle, Valhalla. Just to be certain they were in the right place, Nehor set his whiskers spinning and carved a shaft straight up through the ceiling of roots until he reached the surface of the Dark Kingdom. He poked his head out of the narrow hole and looked around; his eyes, so accustomed to the dimness of the tunnels, were quick to adjust to the darkness. At first he could see nothing but dry, gray ground and skeleton-like trees. With a grunt and a groan, he pivoted his body around until he was facing the other direction. There, right before his eyes, stood the crumbling stone structure that Hasbadana called home. A faint glow from wall-mounted torches emanated from the windows, the only tiny source of light in this foreboding kingdom.

With the skill of an architect, Nehor used his keen sense of direction and distance to mentally compute how far he needed to go underground to reach the center of the castle. Satisfied that he knew where to build the healing room, he pushed himself down the narrow shaft and dropped to the floor where his team of workers waited, landing with an *oomph* on his ample bottom.

Pointing in the direction he now knew they needed to go, he led the diggers down the tunnel. The work began in earnest. Had anyone been watching from the castle windows, they would have noticed a mound gradually arising as the Rodorix below the surface of the ground pushed the dirt and stones around and shoved the extra dirt into a giant pile that forced the ground of the Dark Kingdom up into a cracked knoll. Fortunately, no one in Valhalla noticed.

****

Once Mastis returned from his work on the earth, he, Portlas, Nick, and Lazari met with the Council of the Twelve Ancients in their council chambers. Junia and Gidoni were in attendance as well.

Helam spoke first. "It is our understanding that work has begun in the Underground Kingdom."

"Yes," responded Gidoni. "Animara said they were getting organized even as he left."

Helam turned to Portlas. "Then it is time for you to leave us, dear Portlas. Are you prepared?"

Portlas bowed. He stood back up and looked at each of the council members. "I don't mind telling you that I am filled with no small amount of trepidation. But I have volunteered for this duty because I believe I may be the only one who can succeed in persuading Hasbadana to come with me into the Underground Kingdom."

"Let us give you our blessing to take with you," said Helam.

"I would like that very much," said Portlas with a humble bow.

One by one, each of the council members stepped forward and touched Portlas on the right shoulder, then the left shoulder, then the tip of his horn. As they did so, the light radiating from Portlas intensified.

"Now we must cover you with a shield of darkness to conceal your light," said Helam. Urijah's dependable counselor reared up on his back legs and spun his horn in a wide circle. A ribbon of darkness flowed softly out of the tip of his horn and settled itself over the bay Clydesdale. Portlas, who had just moments before glowed like the sun, was now dark.

"We send you with our blessing. You will succeed," said Helam.

Portlas bowed deeply then whirled and dashed out the door.

The legion members gathered in the meadow in front of the council chambers to receive their instructions. They listened intently before beginning what they all realized was the most dangerous mission they had ever been asked to perform. All felt varying degrees of apprehension. Nevertheless, they followed Nick and Bethany to the sinkhole in Nick's clearing and leaped with blind faith down the hole.

The Rodorix were there to lead them to their posts. The unicorns followed them, commanding the tunnels to expand when needed to accommodate their large bodies as they went along. The unicorns were amazed at the intricate pattern of rooms and tunnels that they passed through.

They stopped in front of the sparkling white doors of Nebbish's chambers. The doors opened slowly, revealing a red glow from the room within. Nebbish stepped out. Never before had the infamous Legion of the Unicorn been invited into his kingdom, and he wanted to be a part of this historic occasion.

"Welcome, my friends. Welcome to the Underground Kingdom of Mantelia. It is certainly a pleasure to greet such distinguished guests." He smiled, and his pointed nose wrinkled as he did so. "It is an honor for the Rodorix to be a part of such an important mission."

The lord of Mantelia scanned the assemblage of unicorns. His eyes caught sight of Nick and Bethany mounted upon their unicorns and his smile broadened, burying his eyes in folds of skin. "Nicholas and Bethany, the master healers!" he said with excitement in his voice. He stepped forward, around Mastis and up to Lazari and Shema. Nick and Bethany reached down and each took hold of one of Nebbish's outstretched paws.

"Hello, Nebbish," said Bethany and Nick together.

"My dear friends," said Nebbish, admiration evident in his voice. "It seems trouble is always either close ahead of or close behind you. Tell me, what will it be this time?"

"We hope this will put an end to our troubles," said Nick solemnly.

Mastis stepped up beside them. "My Lord Nebbish, I am the unicorn Mastis. These are the members of the Legion of the Unicorn. It pleases us to be working as your partners on this undertaking." The beautiful dapple-gray unicorn bowed and touched the tip of his horn to the ground at Nebbish's feet. "Tell me, how are the work teams doing mining the amethyst?"

"The reports are mixed. Some have found extensive veins of pure specimens. Others have not. They have been delivering their collections to the cavern that has been dug for the chamber. You will see the results of their work when you arrive there."

Looking back and forth at the many tunnels that extended away from Nebbish's chamber, Mastis asked, "And which way would that be?"

Nebbish chuckled. "It is not so confusing to the Rodorix. We have lived in the Underground Kingdom all of our lives. Your guides will take you there momentarily. However, before you depart to inspect the healing room, I would like to reiterate the only requirement that I insisted upon from the onset of this cooperative endeavor. My kingdom of Mantelia must be kept safe"—he paused and looked deeply into Mastis's eyes before continuing—"at all costs. Do I make myself clear?"

"Perfectly, Lord Nebbish. That is why we are here. We will do whatever it takes to ensure that you and your subjects will be kept out of harm's way." Lifting the tension a little, Mastis added, "Hopefully our plan will work smoothly and no one will be in any danger." The unicorns that stood behind Mastis nodded their heads in agreement as a united display of confidence.

"Well, thank you for that assurance," said Nebbish. "I will send you on your way to begin your work." He waved them off before turning around and disappearing behind the sparkling white doors.

The Rodorix, who had been sent to escort the legion members, dashed off down one of the dark tunnels. Mastis motioned for his companions to follow him, commanded the tunnels to expand to enable them to pass through, and ran to catch up to the Rodorix. In just a short time, Mastis came to a junction in the tunnels. He stopped and looked down each. He saw nothing. He walked to the entrance of each tunnel and called out. His voice echoed off the dirt and stone walls before being absorbed by the roots above. But there was no answer. Mastis snorted and shook his long mane. "I didn't see which way they went. I suppose we shall just have to wait here until they notice that we are not behind them and return to retrieve us." The other unicorns nodded or let out a soft whinny in agreement. All the legion members settled in to wait.

The wait was longer than they expected but more beneficial than anticipated. When the Rodorix returned, they were carrying large bowls of Mantelia nectar, the delicious drink the Rodorix make from blending the sap of the roots of every plant. Each of the unicorns drank and then drank again. It was possibly the most delicious beverage they had ever tasted, and they said so in a variety of appreciative superlatives.

Once the Rodorix were convinced that their honored guests had consumed their fill, they beckoned them to follow and started down one of the tunnels. The Rodorix were not nearly as swift as the unicorns but had the advantage of familiarity. In addition to that, Mastis had to take the time at every turn to expand the tunnels to fit their much larger bodies. The Rodorix stayed close to them this time and guided them from cavern to cavern and through tunnel after tunnel.

At last, the Rodorix came to a stop in front of a rough-hewn stone room. They stepped aside, motioned with their short front legs to let the unicorns enter first, and said, "This is the room we have dug. You will notice the large pile of amethyst in the center. We hope that will be enough." They waited as, a few at a time, the unicorns entered to inspect their work.

Mastis spoke for the legion members. "This will be perfect. Thank you. We will attach the amethyst, and the room will be ready."

Slowly and methodically, the unicorns used their powers to command the elements to attach crystals to every surface of the chamber. Once they were done, they imbued the lavender crystals with their own internal light. The finished product was something wondrous to behold. The entire room was covered from floor to ceiling with the lovely crystals that glowed with a beautiful, pale purple light.

"It is perfect, simply perfect," whispered Bethany in awe.

"Yes, it is, isn't it," said Nick with a smile. They shut the door and sent the legion members off to take up their stations behind every bend in the tunnels. Most of them were paired up with a Rodorix who struggled to get up on their backs. One by one, the light radiating from the unicorns went out as they called upon the power of the invisible clover.

****

Portlas was intimately familiar with the Dark Kingdom, and he knew the most direct route to Valhalla. With the speed of light, he galloped through the darkness. When he was nearly halfway there, he was stopped by a group of dark unicorns. "Well, well, well, what have we here?" said Shazba, the commander that had replaced Portlas and Salamite as the head of Hasbadana's army. The new commander paced back and forth in front of him.

"Hello, Shazba. It is not you I have come to see. I have some important information to deliver to Hasbadana."

"Oh, I am sure you do. Why don't you give it to me and I will relay it to him? Then we can save you the trouble of traveling all that way," Shazba said with a scornful smile on his dark face.

"Thank you, but no. This is something I must do myself . . . penitence if you will."

"Well, I must say you are certainly in need of that!" he said, and his followers chuckled. "We will escort you to Valhalla."

"If you desire. In fact, I would welcome the company," said Portlas.

When Portlas arrived at Valhalla, he was shocked at its appearance. The castle was even more deteriorated and dilapidated than it had been when he frequented its halls. The few flaming torches that were attached to the walls cast off very little light. Most of it was absorbed by the cold darkness all around them.

Portlas came to a stop in the center of the round antechamber and waited for his host. Above him, a mist of darkness swirled ominously around the dome. Doubt, Discouragement, Despair, Deceit, and Domination, the five pillars representing the Dark Unicorns' virtues, surrounded him. The five columns felt like they were leaning over toward him and would surely crush him if he remained much longer. Fortunately, he didn't have to wait long. The large doors in front of him scraped loudly on their rusted hinges as they opened. The lord of the Dark Kingdom stepped through them. Hasbadana, looking larger and more foreboding than ever, walked forward. Portlas caught his breath but immediately calmed himself by calling on the power of love within him.

Hasbadana stepped up to him then slowly circled him, carefully examining the dark body, as though looking for a chink in the armor. Returning to face him he said, "Portlas, my onetime friend. To what do I owe this dubious honor?"

"Hello, Hasbadana. I have some important information to give you, but"—and he turned his head and looked back at Shazba—"I would like to give it to you in private."

Shazba snorted, "I'm sure you would!"

Hasbadana snapped his head around and glared at his army commander. Shazba lowered his head and stepped back. Hasbadana turned back to face Portlas. "So, here you are, standing before me as you did in days gone by. The result of that previous visit might best be relegated to the 'No good deed goes unpunished' category. I allowed you to return after your traitorous act and you thanked me for my willingness to forgive your transgression by destroying my first attempt to fulfill my destiny. Tell me why I shouldn't just cast you into the dungeon beside your lord and master, Urijah?"

"I don't have an answer for that . . . perhaps you should. In which case, I would not be so inclined to give to you the information that I have collected."

Hasbadana looked at him for a moment. He admired this unicorn's self-serving attitude . . . an outlook on life to which he could relate. It appeared from the darkness of his body that he had not been fully ingratiated into Celestia. At the same time, Hasbadana was certainly curious about the information that Portlas had come so far and risked so much to give him. "Follow me," Hasbadana said to Portlas with a grandfatherly tone in his voice. Shazba glared at them both as he watched them go.

Portlas walked behind him into his chambers. The walls were covered with tapestries depicting Hasbadana in his glory days as the battle horse for Alexander the Great. In each of the works of art, Hasbadana was depicted larger and stronger than his opponents. His rider was holding his sword aloft while Hasbadana fearlessly charged their adversary. Portlas had seen these many times before, just as he had heard Hasbadana brag of his accomplishments many times before.

Hasbadana stopped in the middle of the dimly lit room in front of a pile of overstuffed cushions. He pawed at the pillows until he was happy with the arrangement and lowered his large, angular body down onto them. He turned to face Portlas as he sprawled languorously on the soft bedding. "So, tell me what you have traveled so far to convey," he said slowly, lazily, almost sounding bored.

Turning his head from side to side to make certain they were alone, Portlas began. "Do you know of Nebbish, the lord of the Underground Kingdom?"

"Of course I know of him," Hasbadana said gruffly, insulted that Portlas would insinuate that there was something he *didn't* know.

"Have you heard that he has created a most remarkable chamber?"

Hasbadana pricked his ears forward, clearly curious about where this conversation was going. "What is remarkable about any chamber that that little mole would create?"

"Actually, he's not a mole. He's a Rodorix."

Hasbadana let out a loud snort. "I see no difference. But be that as it may, why would I be interested in his dirty cavity below the earth?"

"It is a chamber made completely of amethyst, and anyone who enters it will be endowed with great power, far beyond his own."

Hasbadana cocked his head and stared at Portlas through narrowed eyes.

Taking the offensive, Portlas said, "Well . . . if you are not interested . . ." and he turned on his haunches.

Hasbadana scrambled up from his pile of pillows, sending feathers floating about the dark room, and rushed around to block Portlas's exit. "What makes you suppose I am not interested? Of course you have piqued my curiosity. Tell me more, but make it worth my time."

"That is really all I know about the chamber. However, I have made contact with Nebbish, and he has agreed to let you see it."

"Why would he do such a thing?" asked Hasbadana, his eyes narrowing with suspicion again.

"I think he wants to test its capabilities. If it can increase your power—you who are already the most powerful creature in all of the kingdoms—he believes all of the Rodorix can become more powerful as well."

Hasbadana walked around the room, considering this. Portlas watched him by turning his head slightly one way, then back to the other. Finally, Hasbadana stopped. "Why should I trust you? After all, our relationship has not been . . . how shall I say it . . . without its moments of deceit."

"That is true," said Portlas. With an air of confidence he added, "You, yourself, said that some lies are justified if they help us reach our objective."

Hasbadana chuckled. "So, you have been studying my techniques and using them to your own advantage, it appears." Hasbadana gave Portlas a sardonic smile. "I must say, I like that about you, Portlas."

"I've done my best to glean knowledge from every source that makes itself available to me," responded the large Clydesdale unicorn. Eager to get back to the purpose of his visit and beginning to feel confident that he had Hasbadana right where he wanted him, Portlas decide to take a final gamble. "But, if you are not interested in my offer, it is no skin off my muzzle. I'll just be on my way then."

"Portlas, Portlas, always the proud one. Did I say I was not intrigued by your message? I just need to contemplate the results if I should become even more powerful than I already am," said Hasbadana with a reassuring tone in his voice and nod of his head. He carefully studied Portlas one last time before responding. "Yes. I believe that I *would* like you to show me this amethyst chamber."

"Then let us go together to the Underground Kingdom."

"And which way should we go to get there?" answered Hasbadana, not wanting to appear ignorant.

"Oh, the Underground Kingdom extends below all of the other kingdoms. We will enter from the lowest level of Valhalla. Can you lead me there?"

A look of skepticism crossed the evil one's face as he cocked his head to one side. "Mantelia is beneath my Valhalla?"

"Yes, and Celestia as well. Can you lead us to the lowest levels of your castle?" Portlas asked again.

"If you are sure that is the best route," responded Hasbadana, still amazed by the apparent vastness of the Underground Kingdom. *Perhaps*, he thought, *I have underestimated those dirty rodents*. He walked across his chambers, past the large tapestries depicting his glory days, and out through the wooden doors. They entered the antechamber with its swirling mist of darkness overhead and turned to the left. Shazba stepped forward, but Hasbadana tossed his head and pressed his ears back, sending the commander of his army back several strides. Hasbadana and Portlas went through an archway alone.

The route they took provided access to one of the round corner bastions of the castle structure. Ramps extended both up to the higher parts of the castle and down to the dungeon. Hasbadana led the way down.

When they reached the lowest level, the ramp ended in a circular stone room. There was no other opening through which they could travel. Hasbadana stopped and turned to

Portlas. "Well, this is the lowest part of the castle. Where might we find an entrée to the Underground Kingdom from this point?"

Without saying a word, Portlas moved past Hasbadana and up to the rough stone wall. He touched his horn to the wall. Immediately, the wall melted away, revealing a continuation of the ramp.

Hasbadana hesitated. "How did you overcome my shields?" he asked suspiciously.

Portlas played the innocent. "What shields? I am merely following the instructions given me by the Rodorix."

"So . . . the Rodorix are more innovative than I had given them credit for, I see. I shall have to make a note of that." Hasbadana stepped forward and gazed down the newly exposed ramp. "The Rodorix actually built this access to my castle?" He found himself filled with an increasing respect for the inhabitants of the Underground Kingdom.

"I suppose so. They have access to all of the kingdoms," he added, thinking quickly on his hooves. Once again, Portlas felt anxious. What if he failed? He immediately pushed the thought out of his head. He simply could not fail. Everyone was counting on him to deliver Hasbadana. He needed to appeal to the dark lord's ego. "I would take it as a compliment that the Rodorix were interested enough in me to invite me to their kingdom. Of course, the choice is yours. But remember, your decisions determine your destiny."

Hasbadana ignored the offensive reference to choice. "Yes, that is true. I will follow you."

Portlas, not wanting to give Hasbadana time to change his mind, stepped immediately through the archway and down the spiraling tunnel. He could hear Hasbadana's hoofbeats and heavy breathing right behind him. The tunnel wound deeper and deeper underground. The stone lining was replaced by walls of crystal. The ceiling was lined with roots that dripped a golden liquid onto the stone surface, making it slick. Both unicorns took their turns slipping, yet they continued to move down farther and farther. With each step, they drew closer to the kingdom of Mantelia.

— chapter 22 —

The Healing

"Heavenly love shall outdo hellish hate."
Milton, *Paradise Lost*, 100

Once they reached the bottom of the ramp, they stepped into one of the Rodorix's tunnels that had been enlarged to fit the unicorns. Nehor stepped up to the two unicorns. "Portlas, I see you have brought a guest with you."

"Yes, Nehor. This is Hasbadana, the lord of the Dark Kingdom."

"Yes. I suspected as much," the Rodorix greeter said curtly. Turning to Hasbadana, the odd-looking animal cocked his head and examined his notorious guest through squinted eyes. "My, my. You are even far more impressive than your reputation that precedes you."

Hasbadana looked down at the Rodorix that addressed him. The lord of the Dark Kingdom snorted before responding in his typical arrogant manner. "Of course I am. And who might you be?"

"I am Nehor."

"And where is the lord of the Underground Kingdom? Why is he not here to meet me?"

"Oh, he will be here shortly. I have sent a messenger to inform him of your arrival. May I offer you some refreshment while we await his arrival?" said Nehor, holding out a bowl of Mantelia nectar.

Hasbadana looked at the bowl suspiciously and stepped back. "You first," he said to Portlas.

"Ah, I don't mind if I do. There is nothing in the world as delicious as Mantelia nectar." Portlas lowered his muzzle into the bowl and took a long, loud drink of the delicious golden liquid. He lifted his head and smacked his lips, letting the golden liquid drop off his chin. "Try this, Hasbadana. You are in for quite a treat."

Assured that the drink was safe, Hasbadana dipped his muzzle and took a sip. The moment it reached his tongue, he rolled his eyes with pleasure and sipped again, this time until he had finished off all that was in the bowl. "I must agree with you, Portlas. That is delicious," he said and almost smiled.

At that moment, a scurrying, scratching sound echoed through the tunnels. Two by two, Rodorix guards dressed in white and red uniforms appeared in the opening of the tunnel on the right. As they entered the opening in which Portlas and Hasbadana stood, they split into two lines, one going to the right, the other to the left. They continued marching, their clawed feet scraping on the ground, until they completely encircled the area. With a screeching command, the lead guard cried, "Halt!" The procession of guards came to an immediate stop. The commander continued, "All prepare for the arrival of the lord of the Underground Kingdom."

Nehor lowered himself to the ground until his nose touched the stone floor. Looking over at Portlas and Hasbadana, he loudly cleared his throat. Portlas lowered himself onto one knee. Hasbadana raised his muzzle. "I bow to no one," he said, his voice dripping with arrogance.

At that moment, Nebbish appeared from around a bend in one of the tunnels. Ignoring Hasbadana's failure to show him due respect, he said, "Welcome, great unicorns. Welcome to Mantelia!" He smiled warmly at his guests.

Hasbadana looked down at him, disappointment evident in his eyes. "*You* are Nebbish, the lord of the Underground Kingdom?"

"Yes, that is I," said Nebbish, paying no attention to the not-so-subtle slight. "And you must be the infamous Hasbadana, lord of the Dark Kingdom." Nebbish bent his narrow upper body forward in a Rodorix form of a bow. Hasbadana acknowledged the obeisance as though it was to be expected and did not return it.

Nebbish ignored his rudeness again and said in a cheerful voice, "Well then, shall we get right to the purpose of your visit? Portlas has told you of my miraculous creation?"

"Yes, he has. I must admit I *am* curious."

"I, too, am curious to see if it will be able to increase your already incomparable powers."

Looking around the confusing maze of tunnels, Hasbadana said with impatience evident in his voice, "So, enough of the courtesies. Let's proceed to this chamber of yours."

"I like a creature that is decisive," said Nebbish, still in remarkable control of his emotions for a ruler not accustomed to being treated with rudeness. "Follow me." The lord of Mantelia turned abruptly and started waddling down one of the tunnels. Portlas nodded to Hasbadana, encouraging him to go first.

"After you," said the lord of the Dark Kingdom, still suspicious of this traitor.

"As you wish," said Portlas as he stepped in behind Nebbish.

Unbeknownst to Hasbadana, the chamber was just a short distance away. However, perhaps in an attempt to confuse the evil unicorn or to impress him with the vastness of his kingdom, Nebbish led them in a long, circuitous route until they were nearly back to where they had begun. At each bend and junction of the tunnels, the little party passed a unicorn with a Rodorix mounted on its back hidden by the power of invisibility. As they drew close to Nick and Lazari, the young rider felt the talisman around his neck get warmer and warmer until, as Hasbadana passed directly by them, it felt hot. Nick subconsciously reached up and grasped the beautiful silver medal and held on to it as the evil unicorn walked by.

The two unicorns and their Rodorix escorts walked down the last of the tunnels. Ahead of them a door stood ajar, revealing a room emitting a beautiful lavender-colored light.

The lord of Mantelia stopped in front of the open door to the chamber. "Here is my creation," said Nebbish with a smile that wrinkled his nose and curled his whiskers.

"Interesting," responded Hasbadana.

"If you will just enter and wait, I am sure you will be amazed at what happens," said Nebbish proudly.

Hasbadana looked at his host with an air of skepticism. He paused and looked into the chamber and then back at Nebbish and Portlas. Cautiously, he turned back toward the door and walked slowly into the room. The door slammed shut behind him and he whirled around. There was no way to open the door from the inside. However, the instantaneous rush of anger and fear that filled him was almost immediately removed from his body and absorbed by the amethyst. Hasbadana was filled with an overwhelming sense of peace, a feeling he could not ever remember having before. He realized that he enjoyed the feeling and let himself just stand in the center of the room and experience the sensation.

As he stood quietly, his thoughts drifted back to his colthood. Suddenly he looked up. Standing before him was an apparition of his father. The large black stallion that stood before him appeared as real and as intimidating as he had in life. In his mind, Hasbadana could picture the last time he had seen his father. That was the time that this respected and feared stallion, with ears pinned back, teeth bared, and hooves flying, drove him away from his mother and the only herd he had ever known. He was a mere two-year-old, suddenly alone in the world on the plains of Thessaly.

"Why did you drive me away?" Hasbadana asked, surprised at the calmness in his voice and heart.

"I drove you away because I loved you. It was time for you to make your own way in the world. Had I not driven you away, you would never have become the great Bucephalus."

Hasbadana shook his head. "I do not understand love like that."

"It is a love born of a wish for you to become all that you had the potential to become."

Suddenly, the room was filled with more phantom stallions. Hasbadana recognized them as the sons he, too, had cast out of the herd.

He looked back at his father with a new understanding. All of these centuries he had carried in his heart a deep resentment toward his father. Now he was able to see him with new eyes.

In blue twinkling stars, his father and his sons disappeared as suddenly as they had come. Slowly, calmly, his mind drifted to the men who captured him and took him to Macedonia. All around the chamber, specters of men materialized.

"Why were you so cruel to me?" asked Hasbadana. Again, this was expressed serenely.

"You frightened us. We didn't understand you nor did we know how to communicate with you except by force. We were wrong. The young boy showed us that."

Instantly the men disappeared and a young boy stood in front of him. His hair was blond; his eyes were kind. He reached up his hand as though he were going to stroke Hasbadana's muzzle.

Hasbadana's ears pricked forward. "Alexander?"

"My great Bucephalus," responded the apparition, the love evident in his voice.

"You left me. You abandoned me. I risked my life to protect you and that was my reward?" Hasbadana said with pleading in his voice.

"I didn't abandon you. I wanted to save you. I could not endure the thought of seeing you killed in battle. Every injury you suffered, you suffered for me. But I felt them, too. I felt the pain as though it had been I that was injured. I could not let you die for me. I wanted your last days to be peaceful and happy."

"But they weren't happy. My happiness came from serving you."

"I understand that now. But at the time, I thought I was doing the right thing. I thought this was the best way to show you how much I loved you. The cities named for you, the holiday in your honor, the paintings, sculptures, and mosaics—all were my attempt to bring you back to me. You, Bucephalus, you were the greatest horse that ever lived. I am humbled that you chose me to be your rider."

A great moan issued from deep within Hasbadana's body. He dropped his head and sobbed great tears of sorrow. The tears eventually changed to tears of remorse. These were followed by tears of humility and finally, after much time, tears of repentance.

The lavender glow of the amethyst grew brighter, and rays of warm purple light moved toward the center of the chamber and surrounded Hasbadana. When the beams of light receded, the giant, dark unicorn was gone. In his place was a pile of dust sitting on the floor.

As though being picked up by a whirlwind, the dust rose into the air and swirled around the room. It dropped to the ground and slid under the door and through the tunnels, passing the unicorns and the Rodorix who all turned their heads in unison and watched it go by. The swirl of dust traveled back the way Hasbadana and Portlas had come from the Dark Kingdom.

Looking like a soft, billowing ribbon of sheer fabric, the dust flowed up the spiraling ramp and entered Valhalla. It streamed down the hallways, pulsating up and down as it passed the dilapidated doors. The stream of particles swooshed down under the only door behind which there was any light.

The dust began swirling in a circle near the ceiling over Urijah's head. The Lord of Celestia slowly, deliberately, lifted his head and pointed his golden unicorn horn at the spinning cloud of dust. A ray of light left the tip of his horn and ignited the dust particles with a sparkling light. The dust began falling, bit-by-bit, to the ground. Four hooves appeared first, followed by pasterns, fetlocks, knees, hocks, a strong chest, and a deep barrel. A thick neck soon supported a large, broad head. Last of all, a long horn formed between the eyes. The eyes were no longer red. One was blue and one was brown.

Urijah looked at him with his soft, warm eyes. "Welcome back, Hasbadana."

"You are free to go. You do not belong here, my lord," said Hasbadana quietly, humbly.

Urijah smiled affectionately. "Neither do you."

****

As he watched the swirl of dust disappear up the ramp, Portlas called out, "Mastis, follow me!" From their hiding places, Mastis, Lazari, Shema, and their riders followed Portlas up the spiraling ramp. Nick and Bethany's talismans were burning against their chests. Nick clutched Lazari's mane tightly to help him keep his balance as they dashed up the slippery stone ramp. When they reached the top, they found the entrance to Valhalla was sealed off. No amount of commanding by the unicorns caused the stones to remove themselves.

Mastis whirled around and charged back down the ramp. He returned moments later with several more unicorns and their Rodorix riders. The Rodorix put their whiskers to work immediately, opening up a new tunnel to the surface. The Legion of the Unicorn members dashed up the opening and found themselves staring at Hasbadana's castle from the outside. The entire structure was shaking. As they watched, the uppermost tower began to sway violently and came crashing down. Nick reached over and grasped Bethany's hand, horror-struck at what they were witnessing. The entire castle began crumbling as rock after rock tipped and fell to the ground before their eyes. The ground rumbled and vibrated beneath their feet. Flames of fire shot up from the center of the castle.

Bethany let out a scream and fell forward onto Shema's neck. Her sobs racked her body. Nick stared wide-eyed at the cloud of dust, smoke, and flames that now arose from the pile of rubble.

Urijah was trapped beneath that mountain of stone. What had happened to him? Were they too late? Had they failed after all? As they watched with their mouths open and eyes wide, the shaking ground stopped. Even the ever-present wind stopped. Everything became still and silent.

Each of the unicorns reared on their hind legs and filled the silence with a mournful whinny. Nick and Bethany sobbed tears of sorrow and frustration as they held on to their unicorns' manes and gripped their barrels with their legs. The unicorns remained standing on their hind legs, pawing the air and crying out in grief and anguish.

Out of the rubble and smoke, two unicorns emerged and walked side-by-side to the top of the pile of stones. Floating gracefully down the side of the huge heap of rubble, manes and tails flowing behind them, the unicorns approached the legion members. The unicorns of light gasped as they realized who it was that was approaching them. Softly and silently Urijah stopped in front of them and lifted his glowing horn.

"There is color in the darkness. We just need to release it," the Lord of Celestia said in a whisper.

Hasbadana followed Urijah's example by raising his horn as well and placing the tip against the sparkling horn of his savior. One by one, all of the unicorns lowered their front legs to the ground and stepped forward. They joined the circle and touched their horns to Urijah's and Hasbadana's until all of their horns were raised together in a salute. A halo of light arose from the tips of their united horns and spread out until it covered the entire Dark Kingdom.

Because of their united power, from this moment onward, color and light replaced the darkness. Instantly, as though awaiting their long anticipated release, tiny buds began to appear on the skeleton trees. Light green blades of grass grew up between the cracks in the parched soil. The wind, which had earlier ceased its relentless blowing, softly blew warm air across the land. The mountains and hills sang with joy.

The unicorns lowered their horns. Hasbadana looked at Urijah. "My lord, I have created much injury in the souls of the dark unicorns."

"Yes, Hasbadana. Each of us influences those around us for good or ill."

"Will you help me undo that damage?"

"Of course, and I have the power of the entire legion to help as well."

Out of the entrance to the Underground Kingdom, unicorn after unicorn arose from beneath the ground. At the same time, several Rodorix chins rested on the edge of the hole, eager to see all that was transpiring. The tips of their whiskers glowed with colored lights.

Walking slowly, heads bowed, tails dragging behind them, the members of Hasbadana's army approached the group of legion members. One by one, the unicorns were given the choice to be healed of their anger or remain an outcast. In the presence of so much love, not one chose to remain in a world devoid of such awesome power.

Once the army was healed, Urijah looked around for Hasbadana. He had suddenly disappeared and was nowhere in sight. Bethany stepped up. "I know where he is," she said to Urijah. "Follow me."

Shema carried Bethany as she led the way to the shores of Loveless Lake. Nick and Lazari followed. Hasbadana was standing on the shore, gazing out over the mirror-like surface of the water.

"Hasbadana?" said Urijah softly.

Hasbadana turned and looked at Urijah, tears flowing freely down his cheeks. "I have cast many souls into this lake, cursing them to an eternity as seaunicorns."

"Then now is the time to heal them as well," said Urijah as he stepped up to the water's edge.

Nick suddenly remembered the ghostly unicorns that attacked them as they were returning to Celestia. He watched in amazement as Urijah commanded Loveless Lake to yield up its prisoners.

The lake began to bubble, and white heads appeared above the surface all around the body of water. Slowly the heads moved toward them as legs beneath the surface pulled the bodies through the water. As they got nearer to the edge, their hooves touched ground, and the ghost-like creatures began rising out of the water. Their bodies were pale gray, almost white. Their once hair-covered skin was now bare. No mane grew out of the crest of their necks; no long, flowing hairs extended from their tailbones. The parchment-like covering of their bodies was so thin that one could see every bone that made up their skeletons. They walked onto the shore, dripping water and shivering in the light and warmth that now filled the land once known as the Dark Kingdom.

Bethany and Nick clung to their unicorns, horror-struck at the sight before them. No creature had ever been as pitiful as these.

Urijah stood motionless, not revealing any emotion other than the pain evident in his eyes. He turned to Hasbadana. "Tell me about these unicorns, Hasbadana."

Hasbadana dropped his head and great sobs racked his body. Between sobs, he choked out the words, "These were the unicorns I drew my power from. When I had taken all they had to give, I cast them away into the lake. I had no need for them anymore, and I wanted them out of my sight." He dropped his head toward the ground, his horn supporting the weight of his enormous head.

Urijah closed his eyes for a moment before speaking. He drew in deep, slow breaths. When he opened his eyes and spoke, his voice was quiet and his emotions controlled. "These unicorns will need a great deal of help." He turned to Nick.

"Nicholas and Lazari, please return to the castle and summon all of the legion members."

Nick nodded, and Lazari whirled on his haunches and cantered up the hill to the side of the castle where the legion members were working hard healing the dark unicorns. When the unicorn and his rider returned to the lakeshore, they were accompanied by all of the unicorns that had come through the Underground Kingdom.

The wet specters remained by the edge of the water. They were so unaccustomed to supporting their own weight on land that they were too weak to move. Several had simply crumpled to the ground. Urijah assigned a legion member to each of the pale seaunicorns. Nick and Lazari approached the seaunicorn to whom they had been assigned with some trepidation, remembering their previous encounter with these lake creatures.

Lazari spoke first. "I am Lazari, and this is my rider, Nicholas."

"Yes, I know who you are. I must admit that the last time we met, I and my associates were not very hospitable," said the frail creature without even looking up at them. His voice was no more than a whisper.

Lazari snorted and shook his head. "Never mind that. That is in the past. We are here now to help you if you will let us."

"I would be eternally grateful," said the seaunicorn as he lifted just his eyes to look at them.

He is in need of so much help. Do we have the power to do this? said Nick in his thoughts to Lazari.

Yes, we do. Do not underestimate how strong you have become, my young rider, responded Lazari.

Together, Nick and Lazari focused their attention on the pathetic creature before them. They imagined him as he once was: a strong and beautiful unicorn galloping across the flower-filled plains of Celestia. Beams of light radiated from Nick's talisman and the tips of his fingers. At the same time, another beam shot forth from the tip of Lazari's horn. Immediately, the seaunicorn was surrounded in a shield of light. His head began to lift ever so slowly. Hair grew over his body and was completed with the growth of a long mane and tail. Muscles developed under the skin, and fat filled in the creases until the body was full and plump. When the bubble of light disappeared, a beautiful chestnut unicorn stood gratefully before them, glistening in the sun like a new copper penny.

The reborn creature looked from side to side, examining his restored body. Without saying a word, he stepped up to Lazari. Placing his muzzle against Lazari's, he blew newly warm air into Lazari's nostrils before stepping back and touching his horn to the ground in the unicorn bow. "Thank you for giving me another chance," he said after standing up again.

Nick grasped the beautiful talisman that hung around his neck. It was cool to the touch. They were in no danger, for the Dark Kingdom existed no more.

****

Nick laughed with delight as he and Lazari galloped across the expansive flower-filled meadow. Ahead of him were the complimentary-colored domes of the council chambers: red and green, orange and blue, yellow and purple. Behind him was Mount Elisia, whose summit was the source of the invisible clover. Beneath him was the powerfully moving body of his unicorn. And all around him was the music that always filled the air in Celestia.

Nick closed his eyes and felt his body moving in rhythm with his unicorn's body. He felt Lazari's strong shoulders reaching forward and his powerful haunches pushing from behind. He felt Lazari's mane whipping at his face and chest.

Nick's breathing matched Lazari's. His heart beat together with his unicorn's heart.

The young unicorn rider opened his eyes and looked to his right. Galloping alongside of them was the beautiful girl that he loved, moving as one with her golden unicorn. Bethany looked over at him and gave him a dazzling smile that made her eyes twinkle. Her brown tresses flowed in the wind behind her as her body moved in the rocking motion of her unicorn's gallop. Nick sat up straight on the back of his unicorn, let go of the mane, and threw both hands high in the air with his face turned up toward the ever-present sun.

Soon, he was joined on the other side by Mastis, running stride for stride in unison with Lazari. One by one more members of the Legion of the Unicorn joined him until there were hundreds of unicorns running abreast across the plains of Celestia. They ran in rhythm to the music that filled the air, their hearts united by the power of love.

The Legion of the Unicorn members stopped as one in front of the bejeweled doors of the council chambers. A few unicorns blew air out their nostrils. Others tossed their heads, sending their manes flying. All waited impatiently.

At last, the golden doors opened and a collective gasp went up from the legion members. Side by side, Urijah and Hasbadana stepped through the doors. But what had brought the stunned reaction from the legion members was the young man sitting astride Hasbadana.

Urijah tossed his head and all became silent immediately. "My dear Legion of the Unicorn members, today is a glorious day. Today we will induct into our ranks the third unicorn rider. I would like to introduce to you Alexander, Hasbadana's eternal rider."

THE END

About the Author:

M.J. Evans writes so that you will love to read. As a former middle grade and high school teacher and the mother of five wonderful children, she understands how important reading is to both a happy and a successful life.

In addition to reading and writing, Ms. Evans spends time with her horses in the Colorado Mountains. As she rides, she makes up stories in her head, many of which are about horses! She loves to get letters from her readers and she promises to write back!

Visit the Mist Trilogy website:
www.behindthemist.com

Learn more about noble and great horses throughout history, or share the story of a noble and great horse that you know at the author's blog:
www.themisttrilogy.blogspot.com
Join the conversation on the
Behind the Mist Facebook page or the
North Mystic Facebook page.

Other fiction titles by M.J. Evans:
Behind the Mist – Book One of the Mist Trilogy
Mists of Darkness – Book Two of the Mist Trilogy
North Mystic

Nonfiction titles by Margi Evans
Riding Colorado – Day Trips From Denver With Your Horse
Riding Colorado II – Day Trips From Denver With Your Horse
Riding Colorado III – Day AND Overnight Trips With Your Horse